Not So Far Away

Deborah Pierson Dill

Not So Far Away

COPYRIGHT 2015 by Deborah Pierson Dill

Contact Information: titleadmin@pelicanbookgroup.com

All scripture quotations, unless otherwise indicated, are taken from the Holy Bible, New International Version(R), NIV(R), Copyright 1973, 1978, 1984, 2011 by Biblica, Inc.™ Used by permission of Zondervan. All rights reserved worldwide. www.zondervan.com

Cover Art by *Nicola Martinez*

White Rose Publishing, a division of Pelican Ventures, LLC
www.pelicanbookgroup.com PO Box 1738 *Aztec, NM * 87410

White Rose Publishing Circle and Rosebud logo is a trademark of Pelican Ventures, LLC

Publishing History
First White Rose Edition, 2016
Paperback Edition ISBN 978-1-61116-533-3
Electronic Edition ISBN 978-1-61116-532-6
Published in the United States of America

Dedication

For my family.

What People are Saying

Ransomed Hope

"Ransomed Hope is a rock-solid story with an engaging plot and characters that tug at the heart strings." ~ Mary Manners, best-selling author

Perfect Shelter

"I recommend this book to anyone and encourage all to read it." ~ Brenda Talley, book reviewer

"This books rings with the truth that, though your heart may break, and all may seem lost, there's always a pathway home, to goodness, faith and love." ~ Marianne Evans, award-winning author

The Lord will fight for you; you need only to be still.
~ Exodus 14:14

1

This was the worst part of every day.

Laurel pulled hamburger casserole out of the oven and set it on the stove top as the truck door slammed outside. She took a deep, fortifying breath, gathering plates, knives, forks and napkins along with her courage, stomach churning as she wondered which side of his personality she'd be faced with when he came through the door.

Tommy's footsteps sounded heavy on the front porch. Angry. And the silence when they stopped seethed with fury. Or maybe not. Maybe she just imagined it. But, no. Her heart stopped for a second as she remembered.

This morning Tommy told T.J. to pick up the mess left by a neighbor's dog when it over-turned their garbage can in the night.

Laurel closed her eyes and expelled a breath.

T.J. came home from school with a fever, and a last minute trip to the doctor confirmed her suspicion that he had the flu. She'd sent him to bed, not giving a thought to the mess outside.

Lord, help me…

"T.J.!"

Laurel jumped at Tommy's shout from the living

room, even though she had expected it. Footsteps came down heavy on the old hardwood in the living room.

"Laurel!"

"In the kitchen." She didn't dare not answer. That would only make things worse. Setting the table gave her something to do and provided some activity that would, hopefully, deflect his anger.

"Where's T.J.?" Tommy stalked into the kitchen, shouting despite the fact that there was nowhere in this tiny house one couldn't hear the quietest of whispers. "Why didn't he clean up that mess outside?"

"He's in his room." Laurel kept her voice calm. Not rising to his level of intensity usually cooled him down. Usually. Sometimes it sent him over the edge. It was so hard to tell which way his fury would go. And right here is where it would probably go one way or the other. "He has the flu, so I sent him to bed."

"You just..." Tommy waved an arm, "...sent him to bed?"

"I'll clean up the mess outside after supper." She put two loaded plates on the table alongside napkins and flatware.

"That's right, you will." Tommy grumbled as he grabbed a beer from the refrigerator and took his seat at the table, more expletives streaming out of him. "That boy's not sick, he's just lazy."

"He is sick, Tommy. He has a hundred and three degree temperature, and he can barely stand."

Tommy took that in, seeming to consider it seriously; seeming for an instant to feel some actual fatherly concern for one of his children. "Where's Joshua?" He downed half his beer, temper cooling.

Laurel breathed a quiet sigh of relief and took her seat. "I dropped him off at your mother's when I took

T.J. to the doctor. He's spending the night."

"You took him to the doctor?" Tommy's angry glare struck her seemingly from nowhere, then it pinned her.

"Y...yes," she said, hesitantly. "He had a pretty high fever."

"Did you see Boyd Wendall? Is that the doctor you went to see?"

Too late, Laurel realized her mistake.

"Is T.J. really sick at all, or did you just make it up so you could go see *the doctor*?"

"Tommy—"

"I've seen you with him, Laurel. And it's clear to me that he likes you."

"You haven't seen me with him. I've never been with him."

Tommy's fist came down on the table, and she flinched as dishes rattled.

"Don't lie to me!" He rose from his seat, sending the chair toppling backward as he rounded the table to loom over her. "You think I didn't notice the two of you together last weekend? At the hardware store, where he just *happened* to be at the same time as us? I saw the way he looked at you. And I didn't miss the way you looked at him."

"Tommy, that's—"

"That's what?" He latched onto her arm and pulled her out of her chair, propelling her toward the wall, and then shoving her painfully against it. His hand slid up to her throat.

"That's not true," she said softly.

His hand tightened slightly as his eyes narrowed. It had been stupid of her to bring up the doctor. Her natural inclination to defend T.J. had overridden

3

common sense. She and Tommy had this same fight on Saturday, when they had indeed run into Dr. Wendall at the hardware store and she stopped to chat for a moment. The bruises were healing. But still, she should have known better than to bring it up. Her husband never needed a reason to hold a grudge—even if it was over an imagined offense.

"Is it not?" his voice was low, like a growl.

She shook her head and turned her eyes to the floor so he wouldn't see anything there he could use against her later. The meeting with Dr. Wendall had been innocent. He was the kids' doctor, nothing more. But how could she resist the temptation to stop and converse with a man who always treated her with respect, warmth, and kindness? What was so wrong about interacting with someone who would talk to her instead of swear at her...someone who would shake her hand rather than slap her? Clearly, Tommy had sensed the longing in her heart for dignity and respect, and it terrified her that he could see her feelings so plainly.

His hand slipped up to her jaw and he forced her to look at him, his fingers dug into her flesh and brought the sting of tears; tears which he instantly misinterpreted; probably as guilt.

Laurel didn't even have time to raise her arms in reflex before Tommy's vise-like grip closed around her arms. He threw her to the floor where she slid into chairs and table, overturning dishes and sending at least one crashing to the floor. She scrabbled to her feet, but he was on her again immediately.

"You're nothing but a whore."

"Then what does that make you, Tommy?"

He shoved her hard, and the impact her back

made with the wall nearly took her breath.

"I'm not the one who's been unfaithful in this marriage. I took T.J. to the doctor because he is sick. And I don't know what it is you think you've seen between me and Doctor Wendall, but it's all in your imagination."

Tommy's hand, poised to strike, came down slightly.

"But you've never been faithful to me. And you call me the whore."

There was no point expecting him to see reason, though she prayed daily that he would. And she prayed now as she saw renewed rage contort the face she had once thought so handsome. *Lord, where are you? Deliver me from this, somehow.*

Tommy's hand, curled into a fist this time, drew back, and Laurel squeezed her eyes shut, waiting for the blow. But the sound of a shotgun's action behind them was unmistakable, and it stilled her husband.

T.J. stood in the doorway with the firearm pointed at his father. His color was paler than Laurel had ever seen it, and perspiration filmed his face, but he held the weapon firmly in his lanky arms.

"What do you think you're gonna do with that gun?" Tommy took a step toward T.J., and T.J.'s finger went to the trigger.

Laurel edged her way along the wall until she was as far out of range as possible.

"I'm gonna shoot you with it if you don't leave this house now."

"You think you can kick me out of my own house? Tommy took another step, and T.J. countered by pulling the gun tightly into his shoulder, preparing to fire. "Maybe I'll go to the police and tell them that you pulled a gun on me? That you threatened to shoot me in my own home. Then you can have your very first taste of prison."

"You won't."

"How do you know?"

"Because they'll want to know why, and then you'd have to explain that you were beating up my mother, which won't be hard for them to believe."

Tommy's glare travelled from T.J. to her, where it took on an accusatory aspect, as if this was somehow her fault. A string of profane remarks punctuated each of his footsteps as he stalked back through the house and out the front door, slamming it so hard the walls shook.

T.J. stood, strong and ready with astonishing coolness under the circumstances, until the sound of his father's engine faded into the evening. Then, suddenly, the adrenaline seemed to drain away and he leaned against the wall.

Laurel made it to his side quickly and took the shotgun from his trembling hands. She followed him to the living room, where he pulled back the lace panel and peered out the window. He sank onto the couch, holding out one hand for the gun.

Laurel stared at his outstretched hand, clutching the weapon in both of hers. Only yesterday if he had wanted to handle his father's shotgun she would have absolutely refused to let him. But today, he had saved her with it.

"You should be in bed." Hesitantly, Laurel handed the weapon back to him, and he set it gently on the floor at his feet.

"I'll sleep in here."

She stacked a couple of pillows at one end of the

sofa, and T.J. sank onto them, suddenly a teenage boy again, checking the position of the gun. Laurel spread a quilt over him. "Do you need anything? Are you hungry?"

"No." T.J.'s eyes closed. "Maybe a glass of water."

She went to the kitchen to get him a drink.

"Do you think he'll go to Grandma's?" T.J.'s question followed her.

Laurel knew what he was concerned about. "He'll probably end up there. But I don't think he'll go there first." She took a deep breath and carried the glass of water to T.J, setting it gently on the table beside him. "I'll drive over and get Joshua."

T.J. nodded, eyes drifting closed. Her oldest son had experienced a good share of beatings.

Laurel always stepped in, frequently diverting Tommy's anger to her instead—trying to, anyway. But this was the first time ever that T.J. had stepped in on her behalf, preventing what was turning into an attack that might have left her needing medical attention. She smoothed shaggy brown hair out of her fourteen-year-old's face. He wasn't a man yet. But he wasn't a boy anymore. Laurel had often wondered if the day would ever arrive when her sons would fight back against their father's abuse.

Evidently, today was the day.

~*~

The shrill chirp of the alarm clock woke her. Laurel's hand shot out automatically to silence it before it could wake Tommy. But he wasn't there. Memory edged sleepy fog from her brain as the details of last night's confrontation reemerged.

She pushed to a sitting position, her Bible still clutched against her chest, open to the book of 1 Peter. In the four years since becoming a Christian, she'd spent every day praying that her unbelieving husband might be persuaded by her conduct to turn to Christ. She didn't scold or nag. She didn't insist that he accompany her and the boys to church—not that he would even if she did.

She set the Bible aside and pushed hair behind her ears. Calling him on his infidelities last night was probably not the best way to accomplish her goal. But he always accused her of behaviors he himself was guilty of. And she was so tired of taking the blame.

She pulled on her bathrobe, donned slippers, and stepped into the hall, pausing at the thermostat to bump the temperature up. Maybe it would take the chill off this February morning. This old house was always so cold in the winter.

Joshua sat at the kitchen table eating a bowl of brightly colored cereal as he worked a game of some sort on the back of the box.

"Good morning." Laurel said softly, kissing the top of his head, and then tousling the mop of tobacco brown hair—the same shade as his father's. "How did you sleep?"

"Fine." He shoveled another spoonful into his mouth.

The train blasted its horn as it reached the railroad crossing less than four blocks from the house, and Laurel paused, waited until the noise subsided and allowed them to finish their conversation without raised voices.

"Are you all ready for school?"

"Mm hm." Joshua affirmed as he chewed.

Laurel pulled out all the fixings for a ham and cheese sandwich and got started on his lunch. The bus would be here in about fifteen minutes, and her shift started at the grocery store a half hour after that. T.J. would need to stay home today, and she would spend the entire day at work worrying. She couldn't drop him off at his grandmother's house because that was probably where Tommy was. And after last night's confrontation...she didn't even want to think about what might happen when the two saw each other again. T.J. would have to stay here, and Laurel would just have to hope that Tommy would go to work today.

Lord, please let him go to work today.

Not only would work keep him out of the house until after she got home, the paycheck was always helpful. Tommy worked a lot. And he worked hard. That was something to be thankful for.

The low rumble of the train faded to nothing except the distant sound of the crossing signal which ended a moment later.

Lord, bless him at work today, and change his heart toward You. And please change his heart toward me and the boys, too.

She tucked the sandwich into Joshua's insulated lunch bag alongside a water bottle, pretzels, an orange, and a few chocolate chip cookies. Then she went to the living room to check on T.J.

Her oldest son snored softly, deep in sleep. Sweat filmed his face and saturated the neckline of his t-shirt, and he'd kicked off his cover. His forehead felt cool to her touch, and his eyelids fluttered open.

Laurel sat on the edge of the sofa beside him, handing him a glass of water.

"Feel better?"

He shrugged and chugged the water. "A little."

"Do you feel up to eating something? Some toast?"

He shook his head. "I'll get something in a bit."

Joshua came in, pulling his backpack on over his coat. "I hear the bus."

"OK." Laurel zipped his coat up to his chin, and he promptly lowered it a few inches. "Have a good day." She stood and walked him to the front door. When she opened it, the storm door fogged immediately.

Joshua slipped out, and Laurel wiped away a circle of condensation to watch him walk to the corner bus stop, getting there just as the bus was coming into view.

She didn't know how he did it. She'd never once heard the bus until it was lumbering down the street in front of their house, but Joshua could always hear it a minute or two before it arrived. She wondered what else her boy had heard that she'd hoped to keep concealed.

"Why don't you leave him?"

Laurel sighed silently as Joshua climbed into the bus and found a seat. Then she pushed the front door closed and turned to face T.J.

He sat up, propped against pillows, but still looking weak and ill. His hair was crimped at strange angles, reminding her of the little boy she'd spent the last fourteen years raising, but a few fine whiskers glistened on his jaw renewing her awareness that he wasn't so little anymore. And if he was old enough to seriously ask that question, then he was probably old enough to hear at least a few of her answers.

"Where would we go?"

He lifted one shoulder and pulled the blanket

higher. "I don't know. Somewhere else."

"If we were to leave," Laurel spoke slowly, calling to memory all the times she'd asked herself the same futile question. "We'd have to leave town completely. We'd have to sever all ties with your grandmother, and anybody else we ever knew here. Because if your dad ever found out where we went, he'd come get us and bring us back. I'd have to leave my job here. And jobs are not easy to come by these days, especially for someone like me with no college education."

"I could get a job."

She smiled. "Soon enough, T.J., you'll be old enough to get a job, and then you'll be working for the rest of your life."

Silence fell between them for a moment as the chill settled anew within her soul.

"Uncle Bobby left." T.J.'s voice rose softly to remind her. "And Aunt Hope. They both seem to being doing fine."

"We don't actually know how Aunt Hope is doing." Laurel corrected him. "No one's seen or heard from her since your grandpa's funeral. And then we only saw her from a distance."

"She's doing fine." T.J. insisted. "She's in school. Working on a degree in graphic design."

Laurel sat up straighter. "You've heard from her?"

"We're friends online."

She didn't know why tears sprang, but they did. "And she's OK?"

T.J. just nodded.

"Where is she?"

"I promised her I wouldn't tell."

Laurel nodded, swallowing the scratchy ache in her throat. "Are you connected with your Uncle Bobby, too?"

He shook his head. "No."

The thought of Bobby raised a wave of resentment. She tamped down the emotion, immediately repentant. The last time she'd seen Tommy's brother had been at his father's funeral. He'd looked as good as she'd ever seen him—transformed. And it was clear that his new girlfriend, Meagan, had never seen the violent side of his nature. She had burned with jealousy. Not because she had feelings for her brother-in-law—that had never been the case. But rather because it had seemed so unfair that he should be the one transformed. Tommy had a family, her and the boys, always at the mercy of his unpredictable, violent temper. Why shouldn't he experience the Lord's grace and become a new creation too?

"Son, I pray every day that your father will turn to God. I pray that he will change and that we'll be delivered from his..." She let her voice trail off and shook her head, not even wanting to say the word. "I pray that God will make him into the husband that I've always wanted him to be, and the father that you boys deserve to have. I pray, and I hope. If it could happen to your Uncle Bobby, there's no reason why it can't happen for your father too."

She left unspoken her silent anguish that her prayers remained unanswered and, as far as she could tell, unheard. Maybe drawing close enough to God that He would hear her prayers was too much to ask of Him. She felt like the dog eating the crumbs of His grace that fell from the table where His children dined, and she knew *that* was way more than she deserved.

T.J. nodded and seemed to think for a moment. "I just pray that he'll go away. That he'll leave one day, and we'll never see him again."

Laurel hated that she understood how he felt. Although that was not the nature of her prayers, she could see how their lives would be, if not better, at least peaceful, if Tommy would decide to leave them. She made enough to cover the bills, although Tommy's paychecks certainly made life more comfortable. But his leaving was not what she wanted.

She loved her husband, despite the hateful man he had become. She had committed her life to him fifteen years ago for better or for worse. So she prayed for deliverance—for him and for herself.

T.J.'s eyelids drifted closed as chills began to shake him. He reached for the bottle of ibuprofen she'd brought him last night and took two, then sank back down into the warm comfort of the sofa.

Laurel rose and covered him up, then pressed a kiss to the top of his head. "I have to go to work," she said softly. "Call me if you need anything. OK? I'll come home if you need me to. And I'll come home at lunch and check on you."

He nodded and rolled onto his side. "I'll be fine."

"I love you, son."

"Love you, too."

~*~

He picked her line on purpose.

Boyd Wendall unloaded the contents of his basket onto the conveyor belt and smiled at Laurel as she totaled the order for the customer ahead of him. Two more of the small grocery store's five checkout lanes were open besides hers. But he had picked hers intentionally, and he shouldn't have.

She bid goodbye to the woman ahead of him in line, wishing her a good evening with the sweetest of smiles he'd ever seen. Laurel Kerr's long, dark, loosely braided hair hung over one shoulder. The pink of the sweater she wore accentuated the rosy hue of her lips and cheeks. Her large brown eyes revealed the gentleness he sensed in her soul—gentleness that existed against all odds if the stories of her home life were true. And, deep down, he knew they were. He hadn't missed the garish greens and yellows of healing bruises on arms, neck, collarbone, even her face sometimes. But she'd never come to him for treatment for herself, only for her children when they were ill. Today, there was a small bruise on her jaw, still purple enough to have been recently acquired. Or inflicted.

"You're off early."

He met her eyes, a little startled at her greeting. "Um…no, not really. The office closes at four. I thought I'd stop and pick up a few things on my way home. The fridge is looking kind of bare." As if he needed to explain his presence at a grocery store.

She nodded. "I still have a half-hour to go."

"How's T.J. today?"

"When I went home to check on him at lunch he was about the same. I don't think he's eaten anything since yesterday morning. And now that I think about it, he didn't eat much then." She spoke as she scanned and bagged his purchase without missing a beat. Her hands were scraped and cut in several places. He didn't think they had been yesterday when she'd brought her son to the office, but he couldn't remember.

"I know it worries you when he doesn't eat. But he will. When he's feeling better. Just make sure he gets plenty to drink. And if he's not feeling at least a little better by Monday, bring him back in to see me."

She nodded and smiled. "I will. Thank you, Dr. Wendall." For a moment she met his gaze, and he sensed the same connection he'd felt with her on so many other occasions when their paths had crossed. "You're total today is thirty-seven ninety-five."

Too soon the moment passed, like always. He'd probably only imagined it, anyway. Boyd swiped his debit card through the reader and punched in his PIN. "Please, call me Boyd."

She nodded again, but looked down in a way that seemed to indicate she would never call him anything but "Dr. Wendall." And that was as it should be. She was married.

He took his few bags out and put them into the back seat of his pickup, then slipped inside, started the engine, and drove home.

The thing he appreciated most about small town life was probably the lack of traffic. Rush hour in Blithe Settlement began precisely at five o'clock, and lasted until about five-twenty. That's about how long it took to get from the main drag to the farthest reaches of the town. And it was a far cry from the commute he'd endured in Houston—an hour long if traffic was moving steadily.

Within minutes, Boyd pulled into the garage of his comfortable home and unloaded the grocery bags. The house was quiet except for the rustling of the plastic as he unpacked the milk, the bread, the eggs...

When he finished, he paused beside the island counter and listened to the silent, empty house. A heavy sigh escaped.

When he was a young man, he would wonder

what his life might look like by the time he reached his late thirties. Settled down, that's how he had envisioned himself. With a wife and a few kids, a thriving practice, a beautiful home.

He'd been well on his way to that future by the time he was thirty. With a beautiful fiancée and a good position in a respected group practice, he was certain the future would be just as bright as he expected. But things didn't always go according to plan. He'd learned that lesson the hard way. By the time he was thirty-one his whole plan for the future had completely unraveled, and the damage was irreparable.

Now, his practice was breaking even, if not thriving, and he lived alone in this silent house. And most evenings he spent thinking about Laurel Kerr— beautiful, gentle, married Laurel.

"Lord, please," he whispered, eyes closed and head bowed. "She is the most beautiful woman I've ever seen. She has the sweetest, most gentle spirit. And she's married to the meanest, maybe the most evil, man in town. Father, protect her and her children, and, please, deliver me from these feelings for her."

2

Anxiety had been mounting since she'd arrived home from work.

Every loud, diesel engine that rumbled down the street, every tree branch that scraped the house in the blustery wind caused her heart to stop momentarily. By the time Laurel heard Tommy's truck door slam she'd felt at least a half-dozen moments of paralyzing panic. But he was home now. The sound of the front door opening and closing proved it, and a supernatural calm descended on her, at least for now. Whatever was to come, it would be over soon.

"Joshua, it's time to clear the table now." Her son promptly closed his school books, loaded them into his backpack, and shuffled off to his room.

Tommy's footsteps stopped in the living room where T.J. still slept on the sofa, shotgun laid out on the floor beside him. After a moment's time, they resumed and came her way.

The panic flared fresh with cruel intensity. If he killed her tonight, she would be free, but what would happen to her boys?

Her heart thundered as she loaded three plates and set each one on the table along with flatware. Then she prepared glasses of tea for her and Joshua.

Tommy watched silently from the doorway.

A quick glance at his face revealed an emotion she couldn't define; not really anger, but not the bland, apathetic expression that assured her of an easy night, either.

"Dinner's ready." Her voice faltered and she cleared her throat. Then she called for Joshua, who came and took his seat silently.

Finally, Tommy went to the fridge for his beer, and Laurel sat. She closed her eyes and breathed a prayer for protection as her husband crossed to the table and set the bottle down. But he didn't sit. He just stood silently beside her, warmth from his body radiating towards her until she couldn't breathe. A wary peek revealed his boots against pea-green vinyl, next to her chair.

She flinched hard when he touched her braided hair, and he drew his hand away. She glanced up at him, desperate for this encounter to be over—desperate for the violence to begin so that it could then end.

But instead of delivering a slap or a punch, he went down on one knee beside her. He fingered her braid a second time and raised a hand to brush a wayward strand away from her face, then to touch the silver cross that hung on a chain around her neck.

It took every ounce of self-control she possessed not to flinch again when he laid a hand gently against her cheek.

His gaze surveyed her face as if he'd never really seen it before.

What was this leading to? Her heart continued to pound as she waited for a blow. She needed to keep her composure. Another flinch or drawing away from him could be the thing that set him off, and maybe that's what he wanted—for her to give him a reason to unleash his temper. She closed her eyes, trapped.

His thumb stroked her cheek softly, tenderly. This was not like him at all.

The memory of his first kiss edged its way into her mind. She'd been eighteen years old, and she'd known without a doubt that—wild as he was, violent as she already knew him to be—her love would awaken in him the tenderness she'd felt in that first kiss. Her love could transform him.

He had even said as much. *A girl like you makes a man want to change.*

The summer night had been balmy and clear. She'd had a little too much of the wine she shouldn't have been drinking, and her senses reeled with every tender touch of his hands. And with the sweetest kiss she'd ever had, he had trapped her. She'd been trapped to this day. And now, with the gentle touch of his hand on her cheek, he tightened the snare. Laurel opened her eyes and met his gaze briefly.

No. This wasn't like him. It never had been. On a good day, the best she could expect from him would be indifference. If he came home from work, ate his supper in silence, and then retired to his recliner to watch television for the remainder of the evening, leaving the rest of them alone—that, in her experience, was a really good night.

The tension from Joshua was nearly tangible. His gaze remained fastened on his plate, his hands clenched into fists on either side.

"Laurel."

Shocked tears pooled suddenly as her gaze slid to Tommy's face. How long had it been since her name had sounded like anything other than a curse on his lips? She couldn't remember. But the way he said it now...she heard affection there—totally out-of-character affection.

Lord, can this be?

"I'm sorry."

She blinked at his apology and a tear slipped free and trailed down her cheek.

He wiped it away with his thumb. "I'm sorry," he said again. Tommy had never apologized to her before. For anything. Not even something he had done unintentionally and was clearly sorry for.

She reached out and touched the rich brown hair at his temple, then she pulled her hand back briefly before finally following through and laying it on his shoulder. Maybe she needed to convince herself that he was real, and not merely a vision…a dream, too good to be true.

But he was broad and strong beneath her touch, and very real, and she longed to lean on him, to depend on him. The look on his face communicated nothing but sincerity. If he wasn't really, truly sorry, then this wasn't the same man she'd been married to for the past fifteen years.

She laid her other hand on his other shoulder and nodded her forgiveness.

When he pulled her into his embrace, she didn't resist, but wrapped her arms around his neck, burying her face in his collar so Joshua wouldn't see the desperate emotions that surely played across her face.

"You were right, baby." Maybe he wanted to look her in the eye while he spoke because he tried to push her out of his grasp. But she slid her hands down to his shirt front and clutched at the fabric there, keeping her face buried against his neck. With a deep sigh he relented and let her remain. "I had no right to accuse you. You work hard, and you're a good mother to the boys. And a good wife to me."

He had never spoken so kindly to her before. In all the years she'd known him, he'd never lavished this much affirmation on anyone. Least of all her. She flattened her palms against his chest and felt his beating heart. Had it been just this morning she had prayed his heart would change toward her and the boys?

Now, it looked as if God was answering that prayer.

She wanted to ask him what happened. What made this sudden difference in his attitude toward her? But she couldn't speak.

And then she felt Joshua's arms come around them both and she couldn't contain the sob that broke free.

Finally, she looked up into Tommy's deep brown eyes, finding the sincerity she heard in his voice reflected there.

And Joshua—sweet, stoic Joshua, who had become an expert at avoiding his father's violence...now he clung to Tommy, whose arm came around him in the first affection she'd seen between the two since Joshua had been a baby.

Laurel swiped at her tears, glancing over Tommy's shoulder to find T.J. standing in the doorway. His stony expression told her that he didn't believe a word his father said, and he wanted no part of reconciliation. T.J. met her gaze for a moment, then retrieved the shotgun and went to his room.

Tommy pretended not to notice T.J.'s actions. But a muscle began to twitch along his jaw, like the ticking of a time bomb. Laurel banished the thought.

"Let's eat, before supper gets cold."

Tommy nodded, took his seat, and dug into the food on his plate, not joining Laurel and Joshua for the blessing. But that was OK. This level of change would take some time and getting used to for him. He would come around.

~*~

The strident chirp of the alarm caused her hand to shoot out reflexively to silence it.

Tommy didn't move. He lay on his side facing the opposite wall.

On an impulse, Laurel laid a hand on his bare shoulder, then pressed a soft kiss to his skin. "Good morning," she whispered.

He stirred to life, rolling onto his back, blinking bleary eyes to bring her into focus. "What time is it?"

"Seven."

A disgusted sound came from his throat. "Don't wake me up at seven." He pulled the covers higher and rolled back onto his side. "I don't have to be at the job site 'til nine."

The rebuff stung more than it ordinarily would have. Laurel reached for her robe and pulled it on as she rose. Her hair hung loose in a long, dark, curling mass—the way Tommy used to like it—but a clip had it under control in short order.

She was halfway finished making Joshua's lunch when she realized he wasn't sitting at the kitchen table reading the back of a cereal box as usual. She found him in his room, still in bed. "Joshua?" She crossed to the window and raised the shade.

Her son lay in bed, motionless.

She pulled his covers back and laid a hand on his

shoulder. His skin was burning hot.

"Joshua." She gently shook him and pulled the covers back all the way.

Chills immediately racked his body and he groped for the covers, finding them and pulling them back up to his chin.

Laurel went back to the kitchen to retrieve thermometer, medicine, and water, and then was back at her son's side.

"Mom, what's wrong?" T.J. stood in the doorway, looking still weak, but better than yesterday.

"He has a fever." Laurel checked the thermometer. "A hundred and four." She brushed Joshua's hair away from his face. "Can you sit up and take something?"

The boy pushed himself up and took the fever reducer, water sloshing in the cup as his shaking hands held it, then he sank back down into his pillow and pulled the covers high.

"Does he have to go to the doctor?" T.J.'s wary question had already played through her mind.

If this was the flu, same as T.J. had, it would pass in a week or so. So, there was really no need to stir up Tommy's suspicion by taking Joshua to the doctor. But his fever was so high. Higher than T.J.'s had been. And his symptoms just started sometime in the night. She knew there was something the doctor could give him to lessen the duration and severity of the virus.

Maybe if she told Tommy about going to the doctor first…maybe if she gave him some warning, and if he could just see how ill his son was…maybe he would see reason.

She rose and brushed past T.J. on her way back to her bedroom where Tommy still slept. She sat gingerly on the edge of the bed and touched his shoulder gently again. "Tommy," she said softly.

He raised his arm to shake her hand off. "I said don't wake me up this early."

"Josh is sick."

"Sick?" He didn't even roll over. "You mean sick like T.J.? Who wasn't too sick to threaten to shoot me night before last?"

"His temperature is a hundred and four, Tommy. If I take him to the doctor, they can give him something—"

Tommy came up out of the bed and turned on her. "No. You will not take him to see Boyd Wendall."

"Then *you* take him." Laurel rose and stood her ground. "I won't take him if you don't want me to. But you can. You can get him the medicine he needs, and you won't have to worry about me seeing anyone while I'm there."

Tommy calmed in the face of her compromise. He scrutinized her for a long moment, seeming to consider.

Her heart leapt at the small victory. Just three days ago, this situation would probably already have ended with the back of his hand across her face. Now, he was not only *not* going through the roof at having been awakened too early, he was actually considering the possibility of taking one of his children to get needed medical attention.

Laurel held her breath, waiting, watching his scowl soften as he considered.

She took a chance and laid a hand on his arm.

He glanced down at the gesture with an expression that looked like contempt. "No. He'll be fine." Tommy stalked down the hall to the bathroom and slammed the door. He got dressed for work and left the house without another word.

Laurel sat alone at the kitchen table. As soon as he was gone, she went back to Joshua's room and pressed a kiss to his forehead, noticing with relief that his temperature didn't seem to be quite as high as it had been a half an hour ago.

"His fever's come down." She said to T.J., who stood in the doorway. "You could probably use a bite to eat. Are you hungry?"

T.J. nodded. "I think I could eat something. Maybe just some toast with jelly."

"Come to the kitchen and sit down."

T.J. sank into a chair as Laurel prepared his breakfast as well as a cup of coffee for herself. Her son didn't reiterate the question he had asked yesterday morning. But Laurel knew he still wondered. She wondered herself. After yesterday's apology, she'd felt so certain that her prayers had been answered, that Tommy's heart toward them had changed. But this morning, Tommy seem more like his old self again.

She took a slow sip of the warm brew, noticing for the first time how chilly the house was again this morning. He *seemed* like his old self. But change came slowly sometimes. For years, she had prayed for deliverance. And she would have faith that now was the time. The Lord was changing her husband's heart. And it might be a slow, time consuming process. But she'd waited this long. Surely, a little longer couldn't possibly hurt any worse.

~*~

"Joshua?" Laurel peeked into his room around ten o'clock.

He didn't respond.

She stepped closer and touched the back of her hand to his head. "Oh, my word." She pulled the covers away from his face and pressed her cheek to his as he stirred. How could he be so hot? She reached for the thermometer to take his temperature. This time it was a hundred and five. "Joshua." She gave him a shake. "Can you stand?"

"What?" He raised his head and peered around, squinting against the sunlight streaming in through the window, then he dropped it back to the pillow, eyes shut tight as if he was in agony.

"What hurts, baby?"

"My head and my throat. Everything."

"T.J." She called for his brother, who was there instantly. "Can you help me get him dressed?"

"What's going on?" T.J. brought sweatpants and a t-shirt.

"I'm taking him to the doctor." Laurel urged Joshua to a sitting position and helped him into his clothes. Then, with T.J.'s assistance, she helped him to the car.

No one spoke on the way to the doctor's office, but it felt to Laurel as if they were all of one mind, anticipating the consequences. Tommy had forbidden her to take Joshua. She knew T.J. had overheard the conversation. Joshua was so sick that she hoped he hadn't overheard it. But the boy could hear the bus from blocks away. They all knew she was defying Tommy, and that the outcome would probably be very bad, certainly for her, but possibly for all of them.

Unless the change of heart she'd witnessed last night had been genuine. *Lord, please let it be so.*

Once inside the office, T.J. helped Joshua to a chair

in the waiting room while Laurel checked him in with the receptionist. When she explained how high his fever was, they called her straight to an examining room.

"T.J., help me, please." Laurel said.

Joshua wasn't so weak that he couldn't walk on his own. She didn't need help getting him across the waiting room and down a short hallway. But she did need a witness. She needed someone who could confirm, in the face of Tommy's coming accusations, that nothing inappropriate had happened between her and Dr. Wendall.

T.J. nodded and rose to support his brother.

Once they had Joshua reclining on the examining room table with a nurse checking his vital signs and asking questions about his symptoms, T.J. took a seat on a chair in the corner.

Dr. Wendall entered before the nurse was finished.

"Joshua? Buddy? What's going on?"

Joshua gave a small shrug; eyes squeezed shut as if the light was unbearable.

"How long have you been feeling this way?"

"I've been feeling bad for a few days. But it's way worse today. I didn't tell Mom because T.J. was sick and I didn't want her to have both of us to worry about."

Laurel swallowed down the ache that rose.

The doctor smiled gently. "That was…quite selfless." He gently felt Joshua's neck and palpated his midsection. He had him sit up so he could listen to his heart and lungs, checked his throat. Then he turned to T.J. "How are you feeling today?"

"Better. A little weak."

The doctor crossed to her other son and felt his

neck as well, then he nodded and turned to Laurel. "I think Joshua probably has mono. I need to order a blood test for him. You can pick up the paperwork at the desk and take it to the hospital this morning, and the results should be in by this afternoon."

"Is that what T.J. has, too?"

Dr. Wendall shook his head. "No. I don't think so. There seems to have been an outbreak at the middle school. I've already seen a few other kids his age with it this week."

"Is it serious?"

Dr. Wendall sat on a swivel stool and gestured for her to sit in an adjacent chair. "He should be fine in a couple of weeks. Keep him in bed for a few days, give him plenty of fluids. He can eat what he wants when he's hungry, but he probably won't have much appetite."

Laurel nodded, committing his advice to memory. "Does he need any medicine?"

"Pain reliever for the aches and the fever." Dr. Wendall scribbled a few notes in the file he held. "Beyond that…there's not much you can do aside from making sure he gets plenty of rest."

Relief brought a smile.

"But…" Dr. Wendall's warning tone reined the smile in. "Mono can cause an enlarged spleen, which is susceptible to rupturing. So, you'll need to keep him…from…rough contact with others."

Laurel's smile failed.

The words had been chosen carefully. But she felt the full meaning behind them. Shame flooded her heart and she looked down at the hands folded in her lap. Is that what the whole world thought of her? That she was the beaten down wife of an alcoholic? A woman who needed to be reminded to protect her children? Was that her entire identity? She glanced back into the doctor's face when she felt the warmth of his hand on her shoulder.

His green eyes were filled with compassion and kindness, but not condemnation.

Finally, she nodded.

"So." He stood again and went back to Joshua's side. "No football, or soccer, or any other contact sports." He paused and glanced at T.J. "No wrestling or horsing around between the two of you, either. Not for a few weeks, anyway."

T.J. grinned and nodded.

Laurel pulled her bag onto her shoulder and stood. "Thank you, Dr. Wendall."

The doctor paused and met her gaze for a long moment, looking very much like he had something else to say. Something like...*leave him and take your children with you*. But she didn't need to hear it.

She'd heard it before.

3

It was impossible not to notice the low rumble of the pickup that pulled up to the adjacent diesel pump. Boyd glanced back to the pump which ticked off the dollars as his own gas tank filled. It was also impossible not to notice the glare Tommy Kerr shot at him when he stepped out.

Every time Boyd had ever seen Tommy, the man seemed angry. But now he seemed to seethe. A glance back proved Tommy was, in fact, glowering at him. Maybe it was a trick of the rapidly fading late afternoon light, but the look on his face almost seemed a challenge of some kind, as if his rage was, at this moment, directed at Boyd in particular.

Tommy went to work pumping gasoline, but the glances he kept sending across the pumps were anything but furtive and clearly intended to intimidate.

"How is Joshua feeling?" Boyd asked the question to break the edgy silence more than anything. The kid's test had come back from the lab a few hours ago positive for mononucleosis. He was probably feeling pretty sick.

"You mean T.J.?"

Boyd shook his head and pulled the nozzle from his tank. "No. Your wife brought Joshua in this morning. He was pretty sick." He plucked the receipt from the pump and replaced the gas cap. But the silence coming from Tommy struck him as charged.

Boyd glanced back to find that Tommy's expression had darkened as he tended his own gas tank with the smooth efficiency of a man who was suddenly in a hurry to be somewhere else.

Without another word, Tommy slipped back into his truck and sped out of the lot, tires squealing.

Boyd breathed deeply and shook his head, and then he climbed into his truck and started the engine. So many things about this little town were still such a complete mystery. He'd lived here nearly nine years, and there were family connections among patients he was only just now discovering; ways of doing things that still baffled him. But this was his home now.

The drive to his house wasn't long, though he lived on the outskirts of town in a sprawling neighborhood consisting of homes built on large lots. He had about an acre, and the house, while not new, was more than comfortable.

But it was nothing like the one he'd owned in Houston. There he'd lived in a lavish, gated neighborhood. The house had been new, the grounds beautifully landscaped, the interior decorated to perfection by the woman who was to have shared it all with him...an imposing stone and brick façade, accented with craftsman style details impressed everyone who came to visit. Impressing visitors wasn't a priority. At least, it shouldn't have been. And he had managed to maintain a reasonable level of humility in the face of his professional success—at least he liked to tell himself that he had. Money wasn't everything; he'd always known that. But the luxuries and conveniences it could buy were easy to grow accustomed to.

It had been head knowledge, however, and not heart knowledge. It was easy to say money wasn't the most important thing as long as there was a plentiful supply, and a promising career. But that wasn't his life anymore.

Sure, by Blithe Settlement standards he did well. But was Blithe Settlement really where he wanted to be? And was it the standard by which he wanted to measure his success? Truth was it didn't matter. This is where God had placed him and he would abide.

The evening passed as evenings usually did; a simple supper, a couple of hours of television, then bed. He wasn't fully asleep yet when the piercing tone of his phone woke him. He shook off the sleepy fog and listened as the admission attendant at the hospital informed him that a patient of his had been admitted in serious condition, apparently beaten.

Laurel Kerr.

~*~

Two local police officers and a sheriff's deputy occupied the corridor outside Laurel's exam room. Her sons sat in an out of the way corner while nurses hustled back and forth. The normally sleepy little Blithe County ER hummed with unexpected urgency.

But Boyd strode past all of it with a singular focus.

Laurel lay motionless on an exam table. An immobilization collar accentuated the bloody swollenness of her face. The doctors and nurses on duty tossed a steady stream of questions at her, to which she was responsive. That was good.

"I'm so sorry to bother you, Dr. Wendall."

Boyd started and turned to a young woman at his side.

She'd been stationed behind the registration desk

when he came in. "When I asked her son if there was anyone he wanted me to call, he named you."

Boyd looked over at T.J. who stared vacantly at the floor as he spoke with sheriff's deputy, Justin Barnet.

"I meant family, and I explained that to him. But he insisted I call you." She cast a quick glance in the boys' direction, then back up at him. "It seemed like they'd already been through so much tonight..." Her voice trailed off as her brow furrowed in concern.

"It's fine." Boyd glanced back at Laurel to see the collar come off. That, too, was a good sign. Maybe the trauma wasn't as bad as it looked from here.

"I hated to disturb you—"

He laid a hand on the young receptionist's shoulder. "It's OK. Are the boys all right?"

"They seem to be." The woman took a breath and let it out on a troubled sigh, then inclined her head to the trauma room. "She seems to have taken most of the beating."

Boyd nodded, then turned and followed the corridor until he came to the bank of chairs where T.J. and Joshua sat.

Justin stood at his approach. "T.J. says you saw both the boys at your office this week."

Justin had been Boyd's friend for a few years. Now, the official tone of his voice surprised Boyd, raising a red flag of alarm. Boyd nodded.

"Yes. Actually, I just saw Joshua today."

Joshua leaned against the hard plastic chair, clearly uncomfortable. His head rested against the wall and his eyes were squeezed shut as if even the thought of the fluorescent light overhead caused pain. He should be in bed.

Boyd took the seat next to him, glancing back at

Justin.

"And?"

"And what?" Boyd was certain Justin should know better than to ask about specifics of his patients' care. But there was something in his tone that sounded accusatory. "The boys were ill and their mother brought them to the office."

"So, there was no sign of anything wrong?"

Boyd's heart rate spiked. He didn't want to jump to conclusions, but it sounded very much as if Justin thought he had something to do with this. It seemed as if Justin thought he needed an alibi, or that he should have seen this coming and been able to stop it. A deep breath revealed this reaction for what it was. Boyd had been here before; defending himself against accusations, as if he should be able to predict every outcome simply because he was a doctor. That couldn't be what Justin was doing. Justin was his friend as well as his patient. But Boyd's guard was up now, and he'd keep it up a little longer. He would not go down that road again.

"Yes," he finally responded, "there was something wrong. The boys were sick."

"They were sick." Justin repeated. "That was it?"

"I assure you, Justin, if I had suspected that someone in my office for treatment was there because he'd been beaten up by his father, I would have addressed the situation with the proper authorities."

Justin motioned for Boyd to get up and come with him as he moved a few yards away from Laurel's sons, but T.J.'s attention followed them with hawk-like intensity.

"So," Justin lowered his voice and Boyd drew closer. "Is there something going on between you and

Laurel?"

Boyd glanced back at T.J. who had risen from his seat. "Something like what?"

"Like an affair?"

"What?" His response was louder than he anticipated.

Justin raised a hand in a gesture that was probably meant to calm him down.

But this was beyond his comprehension. "Of course not. Why would you think such a thing?"

"It's what Tommy was accusing her of when police got to the house."

"It's not true." T.J. was at his side before Boyd realized it. "Dad's been accusing her of that for a while now—of her having something going on with Dr. Wendall. I don't know why. Sometimes it's like he just makes stuff up so he'll have a reason to be mad."

"So why did you have the hospital call Dr. Wendall instead of your grandmother?" Justin didn't seem convinced.

"He's our doctor." T.J. shifted his weight, clearly uncomfortable, whether from the line of questioning or the flu, Boyd couldn't tell. "And I trust him. And Grandma never really takes our side. She's especially hard on Mom. I didn't think Mom needed that tonight."

Justin pulled in a deep, heavy breath and pushed it out slowly with a nod. "Ok. Tell me again what happened. You said he came home already mad."

"He came home late. Drunk. And he went straight after Joshua." T.J. shook his head. "He never does that. For some reason he leaves Joshua alone most of the time. But tonight...he came in and went straight to Joshua's room. But Mom stopped him."

"Stopped him, how?" Justin folded his arms and focused on the boy.

T.J. lifted one shoulder and let it drop. "She just...got in between them. And he'd hit her and throw her off, but she'd get up and get between them again. Until he just turned on her. It happened so fast, and he was just all over her. I couldn't find..." The kid stopped talking abruptly and shot his glance to the floor. There was something he wasn't saying.

"So, why do you think he went after your brother, since that's not his normal pattern?"

T.J.'s glance flickered toward Boyd for a second. "I don't know. This morning, Joshua woke up sick. Mom wanted to take him to the doctor. But he—my father—said no. Later, she took Joshua to the doctor anyway. I guess he found out."

Tommy found out.

Boyd barely stifled a groan. He found out when Boyd asked about Joshua at the gas station. He hadn't known, and that's why he suddenly seemed in such a hurry to leave. Boyd rubbed the back of his neck as tension exploded suddenly. It wasn't an issue of him having been able to prevent this. He had caused it. If he simply had not said a word to Tommy Kerr at the gas station, none of this would have happened.

Justin noticed his reaction. "Is there something else?"

"It was me. I saw him at the filling station, and I asked him how Joshua was feeling. I assumed he knew." Boyd shook his head and glanced back toward the examining room where Laurel was. What kind of father would deny his child medical treatment? Especially a child who was so clearly ill? And what kind of man would beat up a woman for taking her

36

sick child to the doctor? He couldn't even imagine such a person. But he'd stood face to face with him a few hours ago and unintentionally triggered this whole event. "I'm sorry, T.J. I'd never have thought something like this would happen."

"It wasn't your fault. It's just how he is."

Boyd gently laid a hand on T.J.'s shoulder and felt the heat of his skin through his t-shirt. A quick touch of the back of his neck confirmed that the boy's temperature was up. And Joshua was probably pretty miserable, too. "These guys should really be resting in bed, Justin. They both have fevers and need looking after."

Justin agreed with a nod. "I'll take them to their grandmother's house."

"What about Mom?"

"I'll keep tabs on her for you." Boyd said, giving T.J.'s shoulder a gentle squeeze. "The hospital won't release her tonight. You and Joshua need to get some sleep."

Sleep. In a safe place where they didn't have to fear a beating. Hopefully, their grandmother's house would be such a place as long as they didn't have to worry about their father showing up.

"What about their father?" Boyd asked quietly.

"He's in lockup tonight. Maybe we can finally get a conviction and put him away for a while."

Justin escorted the boys down the corridor and out the automatic sliding glass door.

The sense of urgency in the hall had calmed, and so had Boyd's nerves. But he couldn't stop replaying the scene at the filling station earlier. If only he hadn't said anything…if he had simply endured Tommy Kerr's scrutiny and gone his way, none of this would have happened.

Or maybe it would have. If Tommy suspected his wife was having an affair, maybe just the sight of him would have sent him home in a rage. But why would Tommy even suspect such a thing?

Boyd dodged a couple of nurses on his way back to the trauma room, getting there in time to meet Laurel's gurney as an orderly pushed it out into the hall.

She craned her neck, scanning the corridor. "Where are my boys?" The question wasn't directed at anyone in particular—more like at anyone who might be listening.

Boyd stepped up and walked beside her. "Justin Barnet took them to their grandmother's house."

"But Tommy—"

"He's in jail. They'll be safe."

She seemed to relax. "Where are they taking me?"

Boyd glanced at the orderly.

"Radiology," he said.

"They're taking you for some X-rays."

She nodded. "Thank you." Her eyes filled with tears and she looked away as if ashamed.

He longed to smooth a lock of her dark hair, or take her hand—to offer the basic human comfort she probably never received from her husband. But he didn't dare, given the accusations her husband had made. He stopped following the gurney as it made a wide turn down another corridor.

No, there was nothing going on between them. Certainly not an affair. But Tommy Kerr had obviously noticed Boyd's admiration of his wife. Misplaced admiration. Perhaps just a soft spot for a pretty woman in a terrible situation. She sparked a dangerous desire in him to rescue and protect. And it must have been those feelings Kerr had detected on occasions when Boyd had stopped Laurel to converse instead of offering a simple "hello" in passing, which would have been more than enough.

He dropped into a waiting room chair and pinched the bridge of his nose, trying to squeeze the image of her battered face out of his mind.

Was he responsible for this? Had his attention to Laurel been the catalyst for this attack? Had it caused others? Or, if not him, might Kerr have fixated on some other imagined infidelity?

Questions battered his mind and his heart. But one thing was certain. Before tonight, he had only rumor and speculation informing him of Kerr's treatment of his family. Now there was proof. And now that he knew without question what he had previously only suspected, he could not stand by and do nothing.

4

It seemed as if every part of her ached. Even before Laurel opened her eyes she felt the pain in her ribs, her right arm, and her face. She peered down at the cast on her arm through the one eye that opened fully. Tommy had kicked her feet out from under her as she fled from him last night. She'd landed hard on that hand and felt something in the wrist snap. Then he kicked her viciously while she was down. But at least she'd kept him off Joshua. Hadn't she?

Daylight streamed in here and there through closed blinds, seeming to illuminate some memories of last night's violence with painful clarity. But so many details eluded her. The last thing she remembered was X-rays and scans, then being moved into a room. Then nothing. A plastic pitcher sat beside a cup on a tray beside her bed. With her good hand she pushed up into a better position, but shattering pain through her chest and midsection nearly took her breath. She squeezed her eyes shut, but that only caused another wave of pain.

"Don't try to move." A deep, kind voice, not much above a whisper, calmed her, but didn't ease the pain. Then the bed hummed to life as it adjusted to a more upright position.

Laurel relaxed, but didn't open her eyes until she heard water pouring.

"Thirsty?" Dr. Wendall smiled warmly, cup in

hand.

She gave a slight nod.

Dr. Wendall slipped a straw into her water and handed it over, and then he settled into a chair in a way that made her think he'd already been there awhile

"You haven't been here all night, have you?" She drank until her parched throat felt a little better. "Thank you."

He shook his head. "No. I've just been here a few minutes. I wanted to check on you."

Humiliation stung, and she looked away. Only yesterday, he had warned her to keep Joshua safe from Tommy. He had, of course, been more diplomatic than to come right out and say it. But the warning was clear. He had never treated the boys because of injuries Tommy had inflicted. He'd never treated her for anything. But he had known about her situation at home.

Laurel adjusted the covers, an awkward task with only one hand, and that one not dominant. It was probably stupid to think that anyone in this town might not know exactly what her home life was like. Her father-in-law had been the town drunk until his death a year and a half ago. It was no stretch to believe that his son had turned out just like him. And nothing about their family life had ever been a well-kept secret.

But Dr. Wendall wasn't from here. Yes, he had been in Blithe Settlement for a number of years. But he wasn't *from* here. And he always seemed so far above the petty small town gossip. Still, he had known. He had warned her. And now how much less would he think of her for not protecting her children?

"So, how am I?"

"The doctor should be here soon to fill you in. But...it seems to me, your injuries will all heal in time."

"What about T.J. and Joshua? Are they OK? Everything happened so fast last night..." She let her voice trail off, a fresh wave of shame bringing the sudden sting of tears. "How could I sleep all night not even knowing if they were hurt?"

Dr. Wendall touched her shoulder gently. "You were probably given something for pain that made you sleepy." His quiet voice offered consolation, not condemnation, and she raised her tearful gaze to his. "And your boys are fine. They're at their grandmother's. I expect she'll bring them to see you today."

"She won't." Laurel shook her head.

Karen Kerr never wanted to see any evidence of her son's violent nature. As long as she didn't see it, then she could pretend it didn't exist, or so it seemed.

"But they'll be OK there." She squeezed her eyes shut, hating to ask, but needing to know. "And Tommy?"

"He's in jail."

That didn't make her feel any better. When he got out, he'd just blame her for all of this. Then his treatment of her and the boys would likely be worse than ever. But, no point in worrying about that now. Let tomorrow worry about itself. She raised fingers to probe at the tender flesh around her wounded eye. "How bad does it look?"

Dr. Wendall drew in a deep breath, seeming troubled, but his gaze gently caressed the curves of her face. "You are beautiful, Laurel." He said finally. "As always. But you might want to wait a day or two to have a look."

Tears that had been so near the surface finally overflowed.

Beautiful? As always? One eye was swollen nearly shut, and she could still taste blood from busted lips. She'd seen herself after beatings only half as bad as yesterday's, and the result was anything but beautiful. Yet, that was the word he'd used, and he seemed to have chosen it deliberately.

Such tenderness wasn't possible, was it? At least, not from a man who didn't want something from her. And what could this doctor, who was so far above her in every way, possibly want from her? The answer was nothing. Dr. Wendall was simply the kindest person she had ever met.

He handed her a tissue, and she dabbed moisture from her eyes and nose, mindful of the tender cuts and bruises that had warped her features. "Thank you, Dr. Wendall."

He regarded her for a long moment with a look she'd seen every time she spoke with him. It was the look he always gave her just before he asked her to call him Boyd. But this time he said nothing. He only nodded.

A knock sounded on the door before it swung open and another doctor entered. This one wore a lab coat indicating he was on duty. He seemed surprised by Dr. Wendall's presence, but the two shook hands.

"Well…" Dr. Wendall turned to face her again. "I should be going. Laurel, let me know if there's anything I can do to help out." He offered a final gentle smile, then he slipped out the door and was gone.

~*~

Laurel leaned close to the mirror and smoothed a hand along one cheekbone. Two weeks had passed since Tommy's last attack, and the swelling in her face was completely gone. The bruises still showed, but every day they were a little less garish. She sucked in a deep breath, testing the soreness in her ribcage. It, too, was better with each day that passed. The broken wrist would be a few weeks yet in healing. But it was as Dr. Wendall had said to her in the hospital: Time would heal her. And then he had called her beautiful. She stood straight and examined her reflection, failing to see beauty there.

Thankfully, the savory aroma of bacon tempted her away from her vanity, and she smiled. The boys had been so accommodating.

A low ponytail was the best she could do with her hair since she had only one free hand, but this was to be her last day home from work, so she would need to do better tomorrow. She cinched her robe around her waist and went to join her sons for breakfast.

T.J. stood at the stove, watching over a skillet of sizzling bacon.

Joshua had a nice stack of toast made. "Morning, Mom." He grinned as he opened the fridge to pull out butter and jelly.

"Should we scramble some eggs?" Laurel rubbed a hand on T.J.'s back.

"I got 'em right here, ready to go when the bacon's done." T.J. lifted a carton of eggs for her inspection.

"When did you boys learn to cook?" She poured a cup of coffee, doctored it with milk and sugar, and then sat at the table.

Moments later the boys joined her.

"T.J., why don't you ask the blessing?"

Her oldest bowed his head, thanked their Lord for a new day, for restored health, for their home, and for the food.

They had so much to be thankful for, despite everything they'd been through.

The silence among them as they ate seemed comfortable. And yet it was charged with an undercurrent of something she couldn't quite name. She wouldn't call it fear or anxiety, but something similar and to a lesser degree.

"Have you heard anything from Dad?" T.J. asked.

Whatever the undercurrent was, T.J. clearly felt it, too, because it was all wrapped up in the fact that Tommy had posted bail—or his mother had—two days after his arrest, and none of them had heard from him since.

Laurel shook her head.

"What will you do?"

Justin Barnet had encouraged her to seek a restraining order against Tommy. She didn't know what good that would do, other than to make his mistreatment of them somehow more illegal. But she didn't see how that would even be possible given the fact that this was his house. And, as it turned out, she wouldn't have to testify against him if she didn't want to. Nor did she have to press any charges. The case against him was strong enough that the state would pursue his conviction without her testimony.

If he didn't skip bail, he could go to prison for up to ten years. That would mean up to ten years of peace for her and the boys. And in those years, Tommy might be able to get the help he needed to finally change.

But none of that would answer T.J.'s question.

"I don't know," she said finally. "I guess I'll wait and see what happens."

T.J. nodded and looked down at his plate. That obviously wasn't what he wanted to hear.

"What would you have me do?"

"Leave." His response hit a desperate note. "While he's gone, let's pack a few things, rent a trailer and go."

"Go where?"

"Anywhere." T.J. put down his fork and gripped the edge of the table.

"So, you'd just want to leave all your friends?"

"We don't have any friends."

Laurel glanced at Joshua, whose expression told the same story.

"Somewhere else we might, though." T.J. insisted.

"Somewhere nobody knows us." Joshua added.

"What about your grandmother?"

"She bailed him out." T.J. rose and took his plate to the sink. "You know whose side she's on."

Laurel looked at T.J., then at Joshua, at a loss as to how she should answer.

Joshua rose and cleared his dishes. "I hear the bus."

Both boys put on their jackets and then hitched backpacks over their shoulders. They kissed her on the cheek as they shuffled past.

She followed them to the front door, watching them amble to the corner bus stop as the yellow school bus lumbered down the street.

T.J. cast a sad glance back at her as he climbed aboard, then the doors closed and the bus moved on.

Laurel had always thought staying with Tommy was the right thing to do, especially since becoming a believer. And since watching the dramatic conversion of Tommy's brother, Bobby, a few years ago, she clung to the hope that the same thing would happen for them. She pushed the door gently closed. When she twisted the toggle that would slide the dead bolt into place her breath caught.

Why had she just locked the door? It wasn't her usual habit. This was a fairly safe town and she'd never feared for her safety while she was home alone. There was no reason to lock her door other than to keep Tommy out. His keys rested in their usual place, on the table by the door. Without them, he wouldn't be able to get in should he decide to come home. And, while the undercurrent at the table a few minutes ago hadn't felt like fear at the time, now it very clearly did.

She pulled her robe closed at the neck to ward off the chill that had settled in the room from the open door. The question she had, until now, only toyed with reverberated in her mind with an intensity she'd never felt.

Were there any circumstances under which it would not be wrong to leave her husband?

Tommy was abusive. The world would say that was more than enough reason, and no one would blame her. No woman should have to live under the authority of a man who regularly beat her up. Should she? But Tommy's attacks didn't happen every day. In fact, a full scale attack like the one from two weeks ago rarely happened at all anymore. Yes, he shoved and slapped and cursed and intimidated. But was that reason enough to pack up her children and leave their home?

Laurel returned to the kitchen and made an awkward attempt at cleaning up the breakfast mess, wondering. "Lord?" She queried. She pulled open a utensil drawer and took a quick inventory. It would be easy to pack what they needed into a few boxes and rent a trailer, like T.J. had suggested. The hard part would be striking out on her own. And where would they go?

The LORD had said to Abram, "Go from your country, your people and your father's household to the land I will show you.

Warmth gathered in her chest and spread down through her arms.

What about Karen?

T.J. pointed out that she'd been the one to bail Tommy out. And he was right when he said she would always take Tommy's side. But she was their grandmother—the only grandmother they had. And they were the only grandchildren she was ever likely to have a meaningful relationship with. Could she just take them away, leaving no word as to their whereabouts?

The warmth grew more intense, like a fire burning in her heart. She opened another drawer and found the phone book. Then she flipped the pages until she found a listing for a trailer rental company.

"What about my job?" she whispered. "What would I do to support my kids?" She shook her head. This could not be what the Lord was leading her to do. This must be her own desire to escape. But she couldn't ignore the fact that both of her boys seemed to want to go too.

"Lord, is this the deliverance you have for me and the boys? Are you leading me to leave my husband?" She sat at the table and bowed her head, pressing folded hands against her brow. "I want to do Your will, Father. I'll do whatever You want me to. If You want me to stay, I'll stay. But if You want me to, I'll pack up my children and take them away to the place You'll show me."

Even as she whispered the prayer, fear of another kind wrapped tendrils around her heart; fear that leaving was exactly what God was leading her to do.

~*~

The late February chill settled into his knuckles. Boyd flexed his fingers, and then shoved cold hands into his jacket pockets. The winter sun had already set, leaving the world dark, but the evening was still young. He leaned against his truck and watched as digital numbers tallied the increasing amount of his gasoline purchase. Dinner at the Prickly Pear hadn't taken nearly long enough to make the rest of the night not drag on for hours. Another quiet Friday night at home.

The pump clicked off, and he reached for it as a car sped recklessly past the pumps, tires screeching to a stop in front of the convenience store. Boyd managed to get the nozzle hung back on the pump even as he glanced twice at Tommy Kerr stepping out from behind the wheel, the store's blazing halogen lamps illuminating him like a spotlight. A tall, blonde woman got out on the passenger side, and the two entered the store, arms around each other like lovers.

Boyd hardly had time to process the fact that he'd seen Kerr, out of jail and with a woman who wasn't his wife, before a large, loud pickup careened into the parking lot, stopping abruptly beside the car Tommy had been driving.

The truck idled noisily in place while Boyd

retrieved his receipt and replaced the gas cap.

But the moment Kerr and the woman came out of the store, the truck door opened and the driver flew out, lunging for Kerr as the woman shrieked for him to stop.

Kerr dropped the bag he carried, and threw a punch that missed its mark by a wide margin. The two men, both clearly intoxicated, scuffled almost comically for a moment.

Boyd reached for his phone and scrolled through his contacts until he landed on the sheriff's department.

"Blithe County Sheriff's Office, this is Elaine."

"Elaine, this is Boyd Wendall."

"Hi, Dr. Wendall. What's up?"

"There's a fight outside the Gas-n-Go—"

A quick succession of three loud pops sent him instinctively to the ground beside his truck even before he realized they were gunshots.

The woman screamed.

"Dr. Wendall?" Elaine's voice came through the phone he'd clutched to his chest. "Boyd? What's going on?"

He pressed the phone to his ear and rose cautiously as the massive truck sped out of the parking lot and onto the highway. "Someone's been shot."

Tommy lay sprawled on the concrete, motionless.

"You?"

"No, I'm fine." Boyd sprinted to the scene. "Send an ambulance."

"Help him!" The blonde fell, screaming, into his arms. "Please!"

"I will." Boyd set her aside and knelt next to Tommy.

He looked dead already. But the sickening gurgling sucking sound coming from his chest confirmed that he wasn't yet.

It looked as if all three shots hit Kerr in the chest. Boyd pressed his hands to the wounds he could see, knowing there was nothing more he could do. At such close range, there would be exit wounds as well, and the rapidly expanding pool of blood on the concrete beneath them confirmed that theory. There was probably nothing the local hospital could do either. Kerr would need a quick transfer to a major trauma center if he was to have any chance at all.

The woman's wailing cries emerged from outside Boyd's swirling thoughts, as did the sound of encroaching sirens.

Tommy's eyes fluttered open and met Boyd's gaze. He moved his lips as if trying to speak, but instead he coughed, sending blood splattering. His eyes widened, and he struggled to push out a barely audible word. "Forgive…"

Forgive? Was he asking Boyd for forgiveness? For what? Not like Tommy had ever actually done anything to Boyd. If anything, Tommy needed to be asking Laurel and his sons for forgiveness, for not being the husband and father he should've been. Boyd looked into Tommy's eyes. Eyes that gave him a soul-searing stare…was that a touch of fear?

And then it hit Boyd.

Could Tommy Kerr be asking God for forgiveness?

Paramedics reached down to take over.

Tommy's eyes closed and his hold on Boyd was broken.

Boyd stood, seeing the whole scene; the blood

soaked ground, his own stained hands and clothes. The front of his shirt and jacket were covered, and he could feel the drying remains of blood spatter on his face.

A voice, male and familiar, rose above the echoing clamor of the scene. "Boyd." A hand touched his shoulder. "Are you OK?" Concern lined the face of Justin Barnet.

Boyd nodded, and the scene snapped back into focus.

"You're not hurt?"

"No. I'm fine."

Justin studied him for a moment, and then nodded. "Don't go anywhere."

The receding adrenaline left him shaking, and he sat on the curb nearby. There was little chance Tommy Kerr could survive his injuries. It would take more than expert medical care to save him. It would take a miracle.

Boyd had done all he could before the paramedics arrived. And all he could do now was pray. But he was torn.

Did he pray for the miracle that would save the man's life? If he survived, Kerr would live on to terrorize his wife and children. If he died, Laurel would be a widow. Either way, there would be pain for her. Once again, Boyd found himself right in the thick of Laurel Kerr's life.

He looked at his bloody hands, palms up, fingers splayed. Then he balled them into fists, closed his eyes and prayed the only thing he dared.

"Your will, Lord."

~*~

T.J.'s textbook closed with a satisfying snap.

Laurel, after putting the last of the dinner dishes away, turned to watch him gather books, papers and folders, and put them into his backpack. Joshua had finished his homework a half hour ago, and now was playing a video game in the living room.

"All done?" Laurel hung the dishtowel on its rack.

"For tonight." T.J. stretched, long arms reaching high. "I have some reading to do. But I'll work on that tomorrow or Sunday."

"Come on to the living room." Her stomach flipped a time or two now that she had made her decision. "There's something I want to talk to you boys about."

Her son rose and followed her, taking a seat beside his brother who finished up a level and turned the game off.

Laurel sat in Tommy's chair across from them, her heart swelling as she took in the sight of them. Against all odds, they had turned out to be good boys. And she wanted them to have every opportunity to become good men as well. With that thought bolstering her flagging confidence, she pressed on. "I've been thinking and praying a lot today about what we talked about at breakfast." Her voice caught and she had to pause. "I think we should leave."

The boys looked at each other, eyes wide, then back to her. Neither one commented for or against her decision. It was as if they both sensed how hard she had wrestled with the idea. But a spark lit both of them up.

"When?" T.J. asked.

"I go back to work tomorrow. I'll give my two weeks' notice."

"Two weeks?" Joshua's disappointment edged out the spark. "He could be back by then."

"He could be." Laurel swallowed. She understood how he felt. Now the decision had been made, she'd just as soon load a trailer and go. "But Sam has been very good to me as long as I've worked for him. I can't just leave with no notice. It would be wrong."

Her youngest heaved a disenchanted sigh, but nodded.

Silence filled the room as the boys absorbed what she'd told them, each wrapped up in his own thoughts. They seemed excited enough now about the news and all the possibilities it promised. But she couldn't help wondering if they would forget and end up resenting her for taking them from their father.

"Where will we go?" Joshua asked.

"Any suggestions?" She wanted to hear where they wanted to go.

"California." Josh's grin was infectious.

"Alaska." T.J. offered.

"Alaska? My goodness." Laurel rose and straightened a blanket and fluffed pillows as best she could with her good arm. "So far away."

"That's kind of the point." T.J. helped Joshua put his game away. "Even if he did figure out where we were, he wouldn't go so far to get us."

No. He wouldn't.

"Are you getting a divorce?"

She looked into Joshua's pensive brown eyes, so very like his father's, minus the hard edge of rage. "Why would I get a divorce?"

He glanced down with half a shrug. "I don't know. Because then maybe you could marry someone else and be happy."

An ache rose sharply along with sudden tears. Laurel turned and rearranged the mantle decorations, hoping the boys wouldn't see the evidence of her broken heart. "I already am married." She said softly. "Even if your father does divorce me, I don't think I'm supposed to get married again. I don't think I get another chance."

"We could ask the pastor." Joshua's innocence astonished her after all they'd been through.

Laurel turned to face him. "We probably don't want to broadcast the news that we're leaving just yet."

He seemed to think about that for a minute, then a sweet smile spread across his face and he nodded.

A loud, purposeful knock on the front door stopped her heart, as if she'd been caught scheming.

T.J. stood, face flushed, looking to her.

Laurel stepped to the front window and pulled the lace panel aside.

A squad car was parked on the curb.

Relief surged because, if it was Tommy on the other side of the door, he wasn't alone. On the other hand, a sheriff's deputy coming to the house had always meant trouble.

She went to the door and slowly unbolted it, heart hammering.

Justin Barnet stood alone on her front stoop.

A moth slipped in the open door and fluttered to the nearest light bulb. The sound of its papery wings was the only noise for a moment that seemed to pass in slow motion while she waited for whatever news he brought.

"Laurel." He finally greeted her. "I need you to come with me to the hospital. Tommy's been shot."

"What?" The response slipped out with a shallow

breath. Joshua and T.J. joined her at the door and stood so close she felt their warmth on either side. Her heart dropped. Maybe it stopped completely. "Is he OK? Will he be OK?"

Justin drew in a deep breath but didn't answer. Instead, he sent a quick glance to the cast on her arm. "I can drive you if you need me to."

The room had grown cold, and Laurel's mind went strangely blank. She didn't know what to say or do. Her whole body trembled. She stood in front of Justin, as if paralyzed by some emotion she couldn't name.

T.J.'s hand came to rest on her shoulder. "Mom?"

Laurel flinched and then nodded, regaining her senses. "Just…let me get some shoes on."

Justin nodded. "I'll wait here."

In a haze, she slipped on a pair of shoes.

T.J. helped her slip her good arm into the sleeve of her coat. He wrapped the garment around her other shoulder and buttoned it for her. Then he looked into her eyes.

Knowledge that this changed everything was mirrored in his eyes. The next thing she was aware of was their arrival at the hospital.

Justin opened the passenger side door of his squad car for her, then opened the back and let the boys out. Then, with a comforting hand pressed firmly to her back, he ushered them through sliding glass and into the emergency corridor.

Another officer was at the other end of the hall speaking quietly with Dr. Wendall. As she approached the officer glanced at her, causing Dr. Wendall to turn her way. Breath caught in her chest and wouldn't move at the sight of him covered with blood. Without thinking, she reached out to him, a sob rising from her core.

Dr. Wendall reciprocated, taking her hand along with what seemed like an inventory of her physical and mental state.

"What did he do?" Laurel choked out.

Justin urged her along, and she turned to him as Dr. Wendall's grasp on her hand let go.

"Did he attack the doctor?"

"No." Justin's voice was low and steady. "Dr. Wendall happened to be at the scene. He was the first responder."

"So, all that blood is Tommy's?"

Justin didn't say anything. But they'd arrived at their destination, and she could see the answer for herself.

Tommy was laid out on a gurney, motionless. Lifeless.

She stepped toward him, her boys on either side, and pressed a trembling hand to her mouth not knowing what to do or say. She had made up her mind to leave him less than an hour ago. Still, her heart shattered at the sight of the lifeless body of the man she'd been married to for fifteen years, the father of her children, the one she had committed to love for better or worse. She reached out and smoothed his hair as grief tore at her soul. There was no more time to pray for him to change and come to Christ. His time was up.

5

A norther had blown in last night, dropping the temperature from chilly to frigid on this first day of March. The change seemed fitting. It suited her frame of mind. Laurel stepped into her mother-in-law's warm living room and slipped out of her coat.

T.J. took it from her and hung it on the rack, then he and Joshua headed down the hallway to a back bedroom where Karen kept books, games, and toys that the boys were too old to enjoy anymore.

She followed her mother-in-law through to the kitchen and headed straight for the coffee maker. A hot cup of coffee would be extremely comforting at the moment. Maybe it would thaw the icy fingers of shock that wound around her heart.

"He looked good, didn't he?" Karen commented.

Laurel fumbled with the coffee can, managing to get it open. She rummaged through the cabinet looking for the filters. "Yes. They did a good job."

The funeral home staff had cleaned Tommy up, dressed him in clothes that Karen picked out, and laid him in the casket she'd picked out as well. He was ready for the funeral tomorrow.

Food had already started arriving here at Karen's house, and a few casseroles managed to make it to Laurel's house before she left. That surprised her. Tommy didn't have any friends that she knew of. But now that she thought about it, most of the food had been delivered by people she attended church with. Laurel tried with her one good hand to separate the filters, but couldn't seem to. The more she tried, the more frustrated she grew until tears gathered and spilled.

Karen took the filter from her and wrapped an arm around her shoulders. "Come and sit down. I'll fix you a cup of coffee."

Laurel was certain that Karen had misinterpreted her tears for grief. Really, Laurel was simply raw, inside and out. Oddly, she'd cried more tears over the fact that she couldn't seem to feel any grief. At least, not grief that her husband was gone. The thing that grieved her most was the fact that he would have no more opportunities to turn his life around, that he had died in darkness, an enemy of God. She took a deep breath, inhaling the aroma of the coffee, letting the Father console her. Tommy hadn't been hers to save.

The front door opened, sending a blast of cold air through the house chilling her again.

"Mama?" A voice from the living room brought a fresh ache.

"Bobby!" Karen nearly dropped a mug of coffee in her haste to greet her son. The good son.

Tommy's brother stepped through the kitchen door, ushering his beautiful wife ahead of him. The two brothers looked so much like each other. Tommy had been a few years older. And his lifestyle had begun to take its toll in recent years. But she would never forget the handsome young man she had loved.

Karen wrapped her arms around this son, her still living son, tears flowing freely for the one who was now gone forever. Then she turned to Bobby's wife, Meagan, with a tight smile and a curt embrace. "Y'all come in and sit down." Karen retrieved the mug she'd so hastily set aside a moment ago and set it on the table in front of Laurel.

Laurel clumsily cradled it in her hands and breathed in the steam. It was warm and fragrant and just as comforting as she'd hoped.

"I'll stand for a bit." Bobby's deep, quiet voice filled the room, but not in the way she remembered. When she'd first joined this family, he had been every bit as wild as his brother, just not quite as mean. He helped Meagan slip out of her coat. "But Meagan might sit for a while."

With her coat gone, Meagan's second trimester belly was plain to see, especially when Bobby ran a hand tenderly across it. He pulled out a chair for her, and she sat.

Laurel flinched when that same hand came to rest on her shoulder. But Bobby didn't draw away. Instead, he waited for her to relax. In the fifteen years she'd known him, Bobby had never once touched her, not even to shake her hand.

Tommy had hated his brother. And they all knew that one touch, no matter how innocent, was all it would have taken to spark a fight that might end in tragedy.

She raised one hand to cover his, and gave a gentle, grateful squeeze.

Everything was different now.

Bobby could lay a comforting hand on her shoulder without incurring his brother's wrath.

Meagan could sit in this kitchen, getting to know her husband's family, without being harassed.

She, T.J. and Joshua would go home tonight, and every night hereafter, to a peaceful, fear free home.

Laurel sipped her coffee as Bobby moved past her and poured a cup for himself and one for Meagan.

Karen excused herself to check on the boys.

Bobby's wife pushed strands of long glossy hair behind an ear, and then ran a hand across her belly.

"Oh, my goodness." Laurel rose quickly. "I'm so sorry. Have you eaten? Are y'all hungry?"

Bobby waved a dismissive hand. "No, we're fine. We'll get something in a little while."

"Meagan, are you sure?" Laurel directed a smile at her. "I was hungry all the time when I was pregnant."

Meagan's answering smile looked sweet. "I could eat a little something."

"Let me heat something for you. The boys will probably want to eat, too. How does pizza pasta casserole sound?"

"It sounds perfect." Meagan said.

Laurel peeked under the foil covers of dishes in the fridge until she found the right one. Then she pulled it out and loaded three plates, and put one in the microwave.

"What about you, Bobby?"

He shook his head and took over resealing the foil when she fumbled with it. But he didn't ask about the cast on her arm. "How are you doing?" he asked instead.

She listened to the hum of the microwave for a moment, not sure how honest to be. But there was no love between the two brothers. Nothing she could say about Tommy would offend or surprise him. "I'm not sure how to feel." Laurel pulled out one plate and started another. She cast a furtive glance down the hall. "The boys and I had decided to leave him the day he died."

Bobby exchanged a glance with Meagan as he handed a heated plate to her. "Where would you go?" Bobby asked.

"T.J. suggested Alaska." Laurel smiled. "We didn't have an actual plan yet. I was thinking of giving my notice at work the next day and from there..." The peculiar emotion she'd been living with since Tommy's death rose suddenly. She pressed a hand to her mouth to contain it. Then, pulling herself together, she exchanged the heated plate in the microwave for the last cold one. "For years I've been praying for deliverance from him and for him." Laurel whispered because Karen would never forgive her if she knew.

Bobby leaned in closer.

"But this is not what I expected...or wanted. Not this way." Laurel stared at the plate on the counter, unable to meet his gaze. But the warmth of his hand on her shoulder encouraged her to look at him.

"You did not cause this," he said. "Your prayers did not cause Tommy to get drunk and then get into a fight in a convenience store parking lot."

"I know. In my head, I know. But I don't understand ...why this way?"

Bobby shrugged and shook his head. "God heard your prayers, Laurel. He knows your heart, and He knew Tommy's. Maybe He knew that Tommy would never change and so He let Tommy's life run its course. And now, you're free. Your boys are free."

Laurel nodded, and a sob nearly broke free. She pressed her forehead to Bobby's shoulder and allowed herself to feel the relief she'd been repressing for days. Her husband was dead. Relief shouldn't be her foremost emotion. Yet it was, along with a double portion of guilt. But Bobby was right. She did not cause what happened to Tommy. Neither did God. And from now on, she would allow herself to feel what she felt. The truth was she had been grieving for fifteen years.

"Mama?"

T.J. stood beside her. So she composed herself and turned to him.

"My goodness, boy." Bobby clapped a hand on his shoulder. "You're nearly as tall as I am."

T.J. grinned, and then the two embraced in the way that men do.

Laurel handed him his plate, then Joshua appeared and let his uncle put him in a playful headlock and ruffle his hair.

"You know that casserole smells good," Bobby said, letting Joshua go and scooping a generous serving onto a clean plate. "I think I'll have some after all."

In moments, they were all seated around the table, and Bobby blessed the food.

Like a normal family.

~*~

The activity in Karen Kerr's front yard seemed better suited to a family reunion than a funeral gathering.

Boyd stepped out of his truck and watched as T.J. and Joshua tossed a football with Tommy's brother, Bobby, the three laughing and shouting at each other as the women looked on from lawn chairs situated close to the house.

The weather was perfect for playing outside. The sun had come out and warmed up the day, making everyone shed sweaters and jackets, don sunglasses, and bask in the sudden spring-like turn, despite the occasion that brought them all together.

Boyd had not attended the funeral. But he wanted to check on Laurel and her boys, and from the looks of things here, they were doing fine.

Laurel raised a hand to shield her eyes from the sun as she looked his way, then she waved him over.

He crossed the yard and joined the women.

"Dr. Wendall." Laurel greeted him with her pretty smile, fair skin flushed from the sun's warmth. "Come sit down."

Boyd reached a hand out to Karen and she took it. "I'm so sorry for your loss, Karen."

The woman's eyes filled, but she smiled. "Thank you. And thank you for everything you did for him...at the end."

Boyd nodded but said nothing, not wanting to utter empty platitudes such as he wished he could have done more, or that Tommy was a good man who would be missed. Boyd had done all that he could, which wasn't much, given the situation. And he wasn't sorry the man was gone. The thought made him cringe. He was sorry for Karen's grief at the loss of her son. He was sorry for any way in which Laurel's life might now be more difficult as a result of her husband's death. But he couldn't be sorry that the man would no longer be around to terrorize his family. He knew, too, that he'd have to ask God's forgiveness for those thoughts. Which brought him back to Tommy Kerr's last word. He'd tell Laurel, when there weren't so many people around.

"I don't know if you've met my sister-in-law," Laurel's voice saved him from his guilty silence. "This is Bobby's wife, Meagan."

Boyd shook Meagan's hand, then sat in the empty chair between Laurel and Karen. "How are your boys feeling?"

"T.J. is back to his usual self." Laurel glanced in their direction in time to watch T.J. go long to catch a pass launched by his uncle. She smiled at the kid's victory shout when he caught it. "Joshua's feeling better, but he still wears out so quickly. He sleeps a lot. I hope it's OK that he's out playing with them. I just couldn't say no to such a treat."

Boyd dragged his gaze from her lovely face to look at the boys. "He looks good. Seems like he's being careful."

"Can I get you something to drink?" Karen asked leaning toward him. "Some tea?"

"Yes. That would be nice. Thank you."

Karen rose and left them.

"How was the service?" Boyd asked watching her depart.

Laurel took in a deep breath and let it out on a sigh. "It was just a simple graveside service. A few people I know from church came. But I didn't expect a big crowd."

Boyd let his gaze travel back to Tommy's brother who laughed and joked with T.J. and Joshua, both of whom were clearly having great fun.

"Karen wanted to have the service at church," Laurel said softly. Sadly. "I let her make all the other arrangements however she wanted. But he never went to church with us. He never had anything good to say about our going. I thought a church service would be…" her voice trailed off and Boyd glanced at her face watching emotion play across it. Finally, she shook her head. "It just wouldn't have been right."

Following an impulse, he laid a comforting hand on her arm.

Laurel didn't look at him, but she swallowed and her eyes teared a little. Then, with the fingers of the broken arm folded across her lap, she gently grazed the back of his hand. The touch lasted a second, but the deliberateness of it sent something whispering through him. Not reflexive like the other night at the hospital when she'd seen him covered in blood and had feared her husband had attacked him, this touch, brief as it was, had been intentional. It had been a covert acceptance of the comfort he offered.

"Thank you, Boyd." Her voice was low and soft, and he glanced sharply in her direction, sure for a moment he had misunderstood her words. It sounded as if she had called him by his first name. A smile curved the corners of her mouth. "Is it all right if I call you Boyd?"

A grin spread before he gave a thought to it, and a laugh slipped out as her smile spread to match his. "I've been trying to get people around here to call me Boyd for years. So, yes, I'd really like it if you would."

"Well, Boyd...thank you. For everything." Her smile faded, but didn't disappear completely. "You've always been so kind to me and the boys. And I know you must have felt caught somewhere in the middle of our mess these past several weeks." She met his gaze and held it as if she wasn't afraid to look at him anymore. "I'm sorry for that."

Karen rejoined them with his glass of tea.

Boyd offered a quiet thank you as she took her seat.

But something in the woman's demeanor had changed. A moment ago, Karen had been the picture of hospitality. Now, she seemed cold and distant as she focused her attention on the boys in the yard.

He sipped his tea and did the same, making small talk with Meagan, shaking Bobby's hand when he came over to say hello, speaking to the boys when they finished their game and passed by him on their way into the house for a drink and a snack. But with Karen's return to the group, the whole mood had shifted, and it didn't take very much longer for Boyd to recognize that she didn't want him there. He finished his tea quickly and rose. "Thank you for the drink, Karen," he said. "And, again, I'm very sorry for your loss."

"Thank you, Dr. Wendall." Her tight lipped smile contradicted her grateful words, almost making them feel sarcastic. "Thank you for stopping by."

Bobby walked with him to the truck, silent until they got there and were out of earshot of the others.

"Thanks for trying to help." Bobby glanced toward Laurel.

"I did what I could. But with three gunshot wounds at close range to the chest, there really wasn't any way to save him."

"I know. He eventually would have either shot someone or would have been shot someday. It's how he lived." Bobby's gaze remained steady on the women.

Laurel and Meagan chatted together, while Karen sat silently watching them.

"Did he happen to say anything?"

"Yes," Boyd almost whispered. "He said one word."

Bobby's glance was inquiring.

"Forgive." Boyd grimaced. "It's all he could

manage to get out. I don't know if he was asking me to forgive him, or perhaps wanted me to tell Laurel to forgive him...or maybe he was asking God to forgive him."

Bobby took a deep breath, tears sparking in his eyes. "I guess we'll never know."

~*~

"Did you enjoy the afternoon?" Karen's question, as much as the tone of her voice struck Laurel like a slap.

Laurel pulled a casserole from the fridge and peeled back the foil, letting the activity cover her for a moment while she decided how to react. Her mother-in-law's vitriolic tone most likely sprang from grief. The thought smoothed hackles that had risen. "What kind of question is that, Karen?" Laurel began filling plates with food destined for the microwave.

"What kind of question is what?" Bobby entered from the hall that led to the room in back where the boys always hung out.

"I was just asking Laurel if she enjoyed herself today." Karen slammed a cabinet door to punctuate the statement.

"I did," Bobby said, filling a glass with ice, then pouring tea over it. "Your boys are great, Laurel. I wish I'd been able to get to know them better when they were younger."

Laurel smiled, a warm glow forming in her chest at Bobby's words of praise.

"Tommy was their father." Karen almost spat the statement, extinguishing the little spark that nearly lit Laurel up.

Bobby stared at his mother for a long moment, clearly astonished by her spiteful manner. He glanced at Laurel who directed her gaze to the floor to cover the coming tears.

"Well, then..." Bobby lowered his tea glass to the table, seeming to choose his next words. "Aren't we blessed that they take after their mother and not their father?"

"Yes, don't they?" Karen's voice trembled with rage, but she didn't yell. She never yelled. "Laughing and playing and carrying on like nothing happened and not three hours after their father's funeral."

A tear slipped free and Laurel raised a hand to wipe it away.

"Oh, now you decide to cry." Karen muttered. "I noticed you weren't crying when Dr. Wendall was here. You were laughing and having a good old time now that your husband isn't around. It's a good thing T.J. and Joshua aren't girls since they take so much after their mother. If they were, they'd be little whores."

Laurel couldn't stifle the gasp that slipped out. In the face of this unexpected verbal assault, her tears dried up. Maybe Tommy's presence had protected her from her mother-in-law's hatefulness. Karen was always so deferential to her sons. Or maybe what seemed like hatefulness was really just grief working its way out. Either way, Laurel would not begin taking abuse from Tommy's mother now that he was gone—now that she was free.

"That's what he called me."

"What?" Karen snapped.

"The night he did this." Laurel raised her sling bound arm. "And cracked four of my ribs. And beat me until my face was so swollen I didn't recognize my own reflection. Remember that night, Karen? The boys had to stay here for a couple of days because I was in the hospital."

Karen turned away, as she always did when confronted with Tommy's nature.

"He called me a whore. He accused me of having an affair with Boyd Wendall just because I took the boys to his office when they were sick. Then he beat me up."

"Then you called the police."

"Yes, Karen. In the middle of the beating I asked him to give me a minute so I could call for help."

"Either way, he ended up in jail. My son ended up in jail."

"It's not like it was the first time. And he would likely still be there if you hadn't bailed him out."

Karen straightened as if Laurel had just plunged a knife into her back.

"And isn't it ironic--since I'm the whore--that the night he died, he was with another woman?"

T.J. and Joshua had come from the back room and stood side by side in the doorway watching the exchange.

Karen turned to face her, her mouth opening and closing as if she couldn't decide what to say next. "Boys..." She finally got one out in a breathless rush. "Y'all go on back."

"They know all of it, Karen. They've lived it their entire lives. Everyone in town knows all of it. It's not the secret you want it to be."

Silence fell hard as Karen looked everywhere but at her.

The boys didn't budge from their spot.

Bobby's jaw muscle worked as his good mood failed completely.

"I'm sorry, Bobby." Laurel whispered. "I'm sorry you had to come back here and get roped back into all this."

He expelled a breath and took a step toward her. "Laurel—"

"Do not touch her!" Karen's hand shot out toward Bobby as if she meant to save him from impending doom. "Do not comfort her. Can't you see what she's doing? Always the little victim, going to church playing on people's sympathies. Manipulating everyone with her sweet disposition. Tommy most of all."

"You know what?" Laurel turned for the living room. "There is absolutely no reason to stay here anymore since Tommy's not here to make me." She grabbed her jacket and purse from the rack, and T.J. was beside her instantly helping her put it on.

"No—" Karen sounded winded. "You can't take the boys away."

"They are my boys." Laurel pulled keys out of her bag. "They take after me. You said so yourself. And we're just going home."

Meagan rose from her quiet spot on the sofa where she'd been avoiding the confrontation in the kitchen.

"Meagan," Laurel said with a sigh. "I enjoyed talking with you this afternoon. I really hope we get to talk again soon. Goodnight."

T.J. stepped out onto the front stoop, and Josh followed, but then turned back to address everyone still in the room. "I called the police."

Karen gasped. "What? On your own father?"

"He was going to kill her, Grandma." Joshua's

voice was barely more than a whisper. "He kept yelling over and over that he was going to kill her. And T.J. couldn't find the shotgun…"

Meagan stepped behind Bobby, pressed her forehead to the back of his shoulder and wrapped an arm around his waist, clearly unable to comprehend such a thing.

But that had just been normal life for Laurel. The slightest pang of envy stabbed at Laurel's heart as Bobby covered Meagan's hand with his own. Why could that same change not have happened for her and Tommy? And even Karen, and Tommy's sisters, Nicole and Hope? Why would the Lord not redeem and deliver this whole family?

Maybe, as Bobby had said, God knew all of their hearts. Maybe they didn't want redemption.

She followed her sons outside without saying more than a brief goodnight. But inside, her heart cried out. *Where are You, Lord? Where have You been through all of this? Why won't You come closer and show Yourself to Karen? Why wouldn't you show Yourself to Tommy? Where are You?*

6

"Mind if I join you?"

Laurel glanced up from her salad and into the smiling green eyes of Boyd Wendall. She'd been so absorbed in her lunch and thumbing through the latest issue of a favorite magazine she hadn't realized he was here. How she missed him, she didn't know. The deli counter was less than ten feet away and he'd been there long enough to purchase his own lunch.

"Oh." She gathered her belongings and made room for him. "Please, do."

"One of the nurses at my office told me the deli here made good sandwiches and salads." He slid into the opposite side of her booth. "I didn't even realize this was here and I'm in here for bread and milk at least once a week. I thought it might be a nice change."

Laurel pushed a wanton strand of hair behind an ear. "It's convenient on days when we're running late in the mornings and I don't have time to make my own lunch. I can get something without having to leave work."

Boyd popped open the plastic container holding his salad, tore open a packet of dressing and poured it over the mixture of lettuce and chicken. He glanced up and studied her for a long moment. The green and white checked shirt he wore played well with his green eyes and his wavy brown hair. Always clean shaven, with a wide, soft mouth and a swoon inducing cleft in his chin, he was a handsome man.

Laurel had never paid close attention to the small details of his appearance, like the beautiful gold watch and expensively cut clothes, the neatly trimmed fingernails and hair. But they stood out now that he was sitting so near with no sick child or emergency to attend to.

She ran a hand down the front of her store apron—faded blue, soft and threadbare in spots from so many wash cycles. It was a fitting symbol of the difference in their social standing.

"So, how are you?" His question stung unexpectedly.

"I'm holding up OK, I guess." Laurel pushed the remains of her salad around with a fork, appetite withering. When he didn't respond with an appropriately benign and socially acceptable platitude, she glanced up to find him waiting.

"I hope you know you can be honest with me."

Laurel cast her glance to the table, the tenderness in his voice so foreign she didn't know how to react. What a burden would be lifted if she truly could speak honestly with someone. And how did he know that the "all together" appearance she strived so hard to maintain was simply a façade? It seemed as if so many people expected her to respond to the turn her life had taken in particular ways. But half the time, she didn't even know how to feel. And she certainly didn't know how to act.

In front of Karen, she felt as if she had to grieve appropriately. And while she could deal a little more honestly with her boys, to show the freedom she sometimes felt in the past couple of weeks would seem somehow disrespectful. Laurel cast a furtive glance at him to find him eating, but no less focused on her. "I got a new car."

His brows drew together and the smallest hint of an amused smile emerged, crinkling the corners of his eyes.

"Well, new to me, anyway. Bobby stayed in town for a week to help me settle a few things. He helped me sell Tommy's truck and that old clunker I used to drive and get something newer. Something paid for." She took a sip from her water bottle and deliberated for a moment while she screwed the lid closed.

He had just told her she could be honest with him, offering comfort as well as safety. And she had told him about her car. But she knew, although she didn't know how, that if she could not trust Boyd, there was no one on this earth who could be trusted.

"I'm relieved," she admitted quietly.

"About the car?"

She shook her head. "That he's gone." Laurel watched him closely, gauging his reaction.

He finished chewing and swallowed, not seeming at all shocked by her admission. Finally, he took a long drink from his bottle, and then nodded. "Me, too."

"What?"

"It was nice of Bobby to stay and lend a hand." Boyd changed the subject instead of explaining. "I didn't know it was like him to be so helpful."

Laurel tried to smile, but an uncomfortable pang of bitterness twinged. "Bobby's not like Tommy. At least not anymore."

"Laurel…"

"I know what you probably think of him. And a few years ago, you would have been right. But he's changed. Really. The Lord has changed him."

Boyd only nodded. He was skeptical, she could tell, and probably for good reason. He'd most likely seen and possibly treated injuries Bobby had inflicted before he came to the Lord.

"I used to pray for deliverance from Tommy. What I wanted was for him to be saved like his brother. Just...miraculously changed..." She let her voice trail away along with the possibility. "I never wanted the deliverance to come this way. I've been feeling like maybe his death was somehow my fault. Bobby said that God knew Tommy's heart, and maybe God knew that Tommy would never change...and that Tommy's death didn't have anything to do with my prayers. But, I don't know." Laurel didn't even know what she hoped to accomplish with this line of conversation other than admitting her truest feelings to another person.

Boyd started to say something, but she interrupted, wanting to get it all out.

"I used to dread supper time." She curled the end of her ponytail around the tips of her fingers. "I'd never know what kind of mood he'd be in...if he'd be angry and looking for any reason to...or if he wouldn't care, and just want to ignore us and be left alone. But now, there's only peace at the end of the day. The kids and I...we sit down and eat supper and clean up and do homework and watch T.V. And there's nothing to be afraid of. It's strange actually. But I still get this...strong sense of...dread. Every day. I think it's just habit."

Boyd lowered his fork. The pained expression on his face made her wonder if she'd been too honest. Maybe he wasn't as perceptive as she thought. Maybe he, like everybody else, wanted her to bounce back, to pick herself up and move on, realizing how much better life should be for her now.

"I'm sorry." She glanced down into the remains of her lunch.

"No." He drew her gaze back to him with a quick touch to the back of her hand. "What do you have to be sorry for?"

She raised one shoulder, and then let it drop. "Maybe all that was too much information. Maybe it was more than you really wanted to know."

"I knew," he said. "I mean, I didn't know the details. But I knew."

She nodded, remembering his admonishment just a few weeks ago when he'd told her to keep Joshua safe from his father's violence, which she'd done to the best of her ability.

"Everybody knows." She whispered, shame sweeping through her like wildfire. "For so many years it's all I've been to people. It's all my sons have been— pitied because of the abuse, shunned because I was foolish enough to marry him and too stupid to leave."

He glanced away. Clearly, he didn't know how to respond, and why would he?

But she was assuming she knew him. Certainly, she knew who he was, and that he was kind and compassionate. She saw him most every week at church, hands raised in worship—an example she longed to follow but never could. Without a doubt, she knew she could trust him. Beyond that, she didn't know anything about him, or anyone for that matter. For so many years she'd kept her distance from everyone, skirting around on the fringes of this community so no one would see her battered heart or her battered body. The desire to know something personal welled up, fast and unstoppable. "Where did you come from?"

His brows drew together. "The office."

She smiled and nearly giggled—an impulse which stunned her to silence. A long moment later, she found her voice again. "No. I mean, where did you live before you came here, to Blithe Settlement?"

"Oh." He drew the syllable out and leaned back. "Houston."

Houston made sense. A big city seemed like the kind of place he'd be from. "Did you have your own practice there, too?"

He shook his head and stretched one arm across the back of the booth. "I was a member of a group practice. I was an internist."

"Was it much different?" Stupid question. Houston was surely vastly different than this little town, offering more possibilities than she could even imagine.

He drew in a deep breath and seemed to drift away for a moment. "I see more kids now. I didn't see many kids in the Houston practice. The work is all on me here. In the group there were four other doctors and two nurse practitioners to share the load. All the overhead here is my responsibility, which makes the salary lower. But, the cost of living isn't as high, so I guess it evens out."

"Why did you move here?"

Boyd let his gaze wander over the store aisles and shelves as if he was deciding either where to start his story or what he needed to pick up on his way out.

She couldn't help but surmise from the difficulty he seemed to be having that it was a story he might rather not tell. "I get my cast off next week." She smiled gently.

His gaze returned to her face. The smile he gave her didn't quite reach his eyes. Clearly, his life hadn't been as golden as she had assumed. He looked grateful for—no, relieved by. the change in subject. "I bet that'll be a relief. How are your ribs feeling?"

"Mostly better. Every so often, I'll stretch too far or turn a certain way, and I'll still feel it. But..." she let her voice trail off with a shrug.

He gathered the remains of his lunch, all business and small talk again, until he thanked her for letting him join her and rose to leave.

Regret washed over her as she watched him go.

A glance at her watch confirmed that her lunch break was over, so she stood and cleared the table. Then she looked to the front of the store to see if she might catch another glimpse of him.

But he was gone.

There was a story he wasn't telling. But she wouldn't push him to confide in her. Some things were hard—nearly impossible—to talk about. No one knew that better than she.

~*~

Boyd had been on his way out of the office for the day when Elaine Barnet called. Her great aunt had burned herself while cooking, and Elaine wanted to know if she could bring her in. But he was the only one at the office who hadn't gone home yet, and it was just as easy—easier maybe—for him to call on Miss Laura at home.

House calls weren't normal procedure. But for Miss Laura, he always made an exception. His motives were not altogether altruistic, however. He suppressed a wry smile as he grabbed his supply bag and stepped out of the truck in front of her house. There would probably be a dinner invitation in it for him, and he always enjoyed Miss Laura's warm, happy home. More so since Justin and Elaine's twins had come along.

The door opened before he reached it, and Elaine met him on the front porch.

"Thank you so much for coming, Dr. Wendall." A denim overall clad preschooler peeked around her legs and grinned. She picked the boy up.

He had long ago given up trying to persuade her to call him by his first name. But her reticence to do so didn't sting quite so much anymore.

"It's not a problem," he said.

"I hope you'll at least stay for dinner."

"I'd love to."

He stepped inside and followed her to the kitchen where Justin, still in uniform, sat at the table beside Miss Laura helping her steep her hand in a bowl of water.

"Miss Laura." Boyd sat down in the chair as Justin vacated it. "What have you been up to?"

"Just cooking dinner, which I hope you'll join us for."

Boyd lifted her hand from the water and she turned it up so he could examine the bright pink splotches on her palm and fingers. He carefully patted her hand dry.

"I grabbed the handle of the iron skillet that Elaine had just taken out of the oven. I knew it was hot, I just don't know what I was thinking."

"Sounds like an honest mistake anyone could have made." It was a minor burn, and it looked as if they had gotten it into the cool water quickly enough to keep it from swelling. There wasn't much he could do for it that they hadn't already done. "Does this mean there's corn bread?"

The other of the twins, a dark haired, blue-eyed beauty, skipped into the room and asked something he couldn't understand. He clearly got that it was a question by the tone of her voice, but the content eluded him.

"Yes, darling," Miss Laura crooned to the child. "I'll be fine. Dr. Wendall will make me all better."

Boyd ripped open a sterile gauze pad and dressed the burn, wrapping it loosely in a bandage. "You can take an over-the-counter pain reliever if it continues to hurt. But it should be all better in a few days."

Dinner was simple; stew, and yes, cornbread. It beat the ham sandwich he would have had at home, and to share a meal with friends made it all the better. This had been the second meal he'd shared with someone today. Maybe the Lord provided his companions today for a reason. It was always hard to have his meals alone. But maybe today would have been harder than normal. Then it hit him. Today was March the twenty-fifth. If things had gone differently, it would have been his wedding anniversary.

Too soon, Miss Laura and Elaine rose to clear the dishes.

Boyd trespassed on their hospitality as long as he dared, making small talk at the table with Justin until Elaine gathered the twins and headed them off for a bath. Then he rose. "I should get going."

Justin walked him to the front porch.

"Listen, I'm sorry if I came across as accusatory a few weeks back—at the hospital. I really wasn't accusing you of anything."

Boyd shook his head and dismissed the apology with a wave of his hand. "You were doing your job."

Justin nodded. "I didn't believe a word of Tommy's accusations. But when T.J. had the hospital call you, it made me wonder."

"I'm sorry; I can't explain why he did that."

"But you don't mind that he did?"

It was hard to tell if Justin was fishing for information as a law enforcement officer, or offering the opportunity to confide as a friend. The uniform he still wore gave more credence to the former possibility rather than the latter. And if there was one thing he knew about Justin, it was that he could never really separate his lawman side from any other part.

"No," Boyd began cautiously. "I didn't mind. Both boys were ill. I figured if they were calling me, they must not have anyone else. And given their mother's injuries, maybe they thought it best to call the doctor they know." He punctuated his theory with a shrug.

Justin listened, his posture and expression informal and unofficial, so Boyd continued, deciding to speak as a friend and trusting that Justin would reciprocate.

"I've admired Laurel for a while. I shouldn't have, I know. And I don't really know if what I feel for her is a real attraction, or if it's compassion, or some combination of both. I don't know her well enough personally to really be able to judge."

Justin leaned on the porch railing, seeming to observe the antics of a cat in the neighbor's yard.

"I'm afraid I might have been the cause of Tommy's anger on an occasion or two. I may have stopped to chat with her when I shouldn't have. But there's never been anything improper or inappropriate between us. Well, other than my completely one-sided attraction to a married woman."

"You were never the cause of Tommy's anger." Justin spoke without looking at him. "He's been mistreating her since the day he met her. No worse since you came along. It's just how that family is."

The question that rose from the incomprehensibleness of her situation was why.

Why had law enforcement not been able to do more to help her? Why had no one been able to convince her to leave her abusive husband? It seemed everyone had the same question and no one knew the answer. Maybe not even Laurel. But if she'd been as isolated by her husband as she seemed, it would make sense that no one wanted to reach out to her. Incurring Tommy's anger could only result in danger, and not wanting to go up against him was understandable. But it still raised a swell of disappointment that no one would even try. But then, neither had he.

"I was sure sorry to see her get tangled up with Tommy Kerr." Justin's quiet assertion drew Boyd back to the conversation. "She came to Blithe Settlement when we were in the…oh, I guess the third or fourth grade. She seemed like a sweet girl. Kind of quiet and shy, but very sweet and kind. It's kind of a miracle that living with Tommy and his family for all these years doesn't seem to have changed that about her. But I don't need to keep you here all night. Thanks for coming to the house." Justin extended his hand, and Boyd shook it. "Miss Laura isn't getting around as well as she used to. Elaine worries about her."

"I'm glad to do it. Call if you need anything. You have my number." Boyd stepped down to the front walk as his phone rang. He pulled the device from his pocket and glanced at the screen as he slid into his truck. The familiar number caused his heart to lurch. Boyd pulled the door closed and accepted the call. "Hello?"

"Boyd? It's Annette." Her voice sounded disturbingly familiar; as if he'd just heard it yesterday. For an instant, he was back in Houston—before anything had ever gone wrong—with his whole life before him. "How are you?"

"I'm all right, Annette. How are you?" He pushed the key into the ignition and started the pickup.

"Are you driving?"

"I'm just leaving a friend's house."

"Are you making a house call?"

She was joking. Actually, she was teasing him about his small town practice. Normally, he could go with it. But it irritated just now. "Yes, actually, I am."

"Oh...well...that's kind of...sweet."

For an uncomfortable moment, there was only silence while he waited for her to begin.

"I ran into your mother last week, and we ended up having lunch together."

Boyd suspected their breakup had been as hard on his parents as it had been on him. They loved Annette. It didn't surprise him that his mother would want to stop and catch up—maybe even lobby for them to reunite.

"I asked her how you were doing, and she said I should just give you a call and ask you for myself. So...how are you?"

A couple of times a year she got the urge to call and catch up. He might understand the need if he had broken up with her. But it hadn't gone that way. She had been the one to end their engagement, and her occasional phone calls—even all these years later—made him feel as if she was keeping him on a back burner in case another doctor never came calling.

"I'm doing all right, Annette."

"Can you talk?"

"Now's not a good time."

It was probably as good a time as any. But there was nothing to say. And he had enough on his mind without trying to decode everything she said.

"Oh." She sounded disappointed. "OK. Well I wanted to let you know that I'll be heading west for a ski vacation in the fall. It turns out Blithe Settlement isn't too far out of the way."

There was a long pause.

Boyd waited.

"Anyway, I thought I might swing through and meet you for lunch or dinner."

"I can't imagine that Blithe Settlement is on the way to anywhere, but if you happened to be passing through, I'd be happy to meet up with you. But you don't need to go out of your way—"

"Great." Her voice brightened. "So, I'll call you closer to the date."

"That'd be fine."

"OK." Another pause. "Well, I'll let you get back to your house call. Talk to you soon."

"Thanks for calling, Annette. Bye." Boyd ended the call and drew in a deep breath, letting it out as he tried to push the suspicion out of his mind. She probably hadn't intended for the way she said *house call* to sound so patronizing. Her father, the plastic surgeon, would never call on a patient at home, so the idea probably sounded like an idea from a previous century. And maybe it was. He glanced back at Miss Laura's house.

It wasn't Houston, but this town was the place of God's provision for him, house calls and all. The plans he'd made for his life hadn't looked remotely like the life he had now. But he clung to his belief that what he had now was somehow part of God's bigger plan for him regardless of how small it felt in this moment. So he would abide.

~*~

Laurel sighed heavily, arriving home from work an hour earlier than usual.

Joshua slumped onto the couch and dropped his backpack to the floor between his feet. Shame colored his face in angry red blotches. The call from the principal had come just after three o'clock. Joshua had been fighting in the bus line—quiet, non-confrontational Joshua.

Laurel shed her wind breaker and hung it on the coat rack.

T.J. sat beside his brother.

"Do you want to tell me what happened?" Laurel asked.

Joshua shrugged.

"Who started it?"

This was a detail the principal hadn't been able to get him to talk about either. Her son had just sat there in the school office, taking the blame. But she knew this son of hers, and she couldn't imagine him starting a fight.

"I hit him first, if that's what you mean." Joshua didn't look at her. "But he started it."

"How, exactly?"

He raised his gaze to hers briefly, then cast it downward again, reluctant to tell her what the other kid had said or done.

"Did he say something? Did he shove you? What?"

"He said something."

"About?"

"About Dad. And you."

"What did he say?"

Joshua shook his head.

So Laurel turned to T.J. "Did you hear what he said?"

T.J. nodded.

"Will you tell me?"

T.J. shook his head. "But if it had been an older kid who said it, I probably would have hit him, too."

"Was it that bad?"

Both boys nodded.

"And you won't tell me?"

Joshua looked at T.J. who shook his head. "It's not important, and it's not true."

"Clearly, it was important if it was worth fighting over."

"It doesn't matter," Joshua said

"And I know what people in this town thought of your father, as well as what they think of me. I promise you, it won't shock me like you think it will."

The boys sat, tight lipped and silent.

"All right." Laurel reached behind her to untie her store apron, managing to slip it off and hanging it with her jacket. With a final, resigned breath, she headed for the kitchen where she opened the pantry and stared at its contents, unseeing. After a long moment, she pulled out a box of spaghetti pasta, tucked it under her casted arm, and then got a jar of sauce.

She closed the pantry and jumped, nearly losing her hold on the spaghetti sauce when she saw Joshua standing just on the other side of the door. "My goodness, Joshua! You scared me half to death."

"So, you won't punish me?"

The burst of adrenaline left her trembling and she crossed to the stove to put the items down before she really did drop them. She took a moment to regain her composure by retrieving a pot and filling it with water. "You got three days' detention, right?"

Joshua took the pot from the sink to the stove. "Yes, ma'am."

"Do you feel like that's not enough punishment?"

He shrugged. "I don't know. Dad would've—"

"Yes, I know." She covered an emotion she couldn't define by turning to the fridge in search of ground beef.

T.J. came to stand in the doorway.

"Your father would have punished you further. He probably would have beaten you up for fighting at school as if he'd never done the exact same thing. And he wouldn't have been the least bit concerned about the reason for the fight."

The color drained from her son's face and his eyes filled suddenly, alarming her.

"Joshua?"

"I'm sorry, Mom." His voice cracked and he cleared his throat. "I'm not gonna turn out like him. I don't want to be like him." He threw his arms around her neck as sobs racked his body suddenly.

"Oh, son." She closed her good arm around him as he wept. "The thought that either one of you boys could ever turn out like him never once crossed my mind. I didn't mean to suggest such a thing." She held him until he was able to compose himself, then she handed him a napkin to clean his face. "Boys fight, honey. That's what I was trying to say. And kids can be mean. Trust me, I know, especially to those who are even a little bit different. And, no, I don't intend to punish you further. You were fighting to defend my honor, and you shouldn't need any more proof than that to know you're nothing like your dad, because that's probably the one thing he would never have fought for."

Joshua nodded, sniffing as he turned to take a seat at the table.

Laurel unwrapped the ground beef and dumped it into a skillet to brown.

How long would Tommy's hold on this family remain? He had only been gone a few weeks, so it was too soon yet for life to feel normal. But what would normal feel like when it finally came? Would the shadow of their abusive father follow T.J. and Joshua their whole lives, or was it something that would fade with time?

"I was reading the Bible the other night." Joshua's voice rose above the increasing sizzle of the cooking meat. "And I found a verse in Exodus. 'Yet he does not leave the guilty unpunished; he punishes the children and their children for the sin of the fathers to the third and fourth generation.' What does that mean for us, Mom?"

Laurel took a deep breath and held it, keenly aware that she had never felt more inept as a parent than at this moment. She herself was fairly new to this faith. And while she understood that Christ had died as a sacrifice to cover her sin, she still grappled daily with the existence of such grace and mercy. There was so much more she didn't understand. How was she to guide her children, whose questions would likely be far more complex, given their lives thus far, than the average kid? But right now, she had to say something. She turned to face him. "Maybe it means that you and your brother will have to live with the consequences of your father's sin for the rest of your lives."

T.J. came and sat with his brother.

"I don't think it means that you are doomed to repeat his sins. But they will affect you, and me, from now on, even though he's gone now."

"What about if we have kids?" T.J. asked.

"I don't know." Laurel sighed, wishing that God were close enough to whisper the answer into her ear, and fearing that He never would be. "Why don't we stay after church on Sunday and ask the pastor? And let's assume that you boys are the fourth generation, and your kids will be free."

7

Laurel didn't know the first thing about bake sales. So why she felt drawn to—even excited about—the opportunity to help with this one, she couldn't say. But last week when Audrey Thomason asked her to not only bake something to sell, but also to help staff the church bake sale table for the Bluebonnet Days Fair, her spirit hummed with optimism. It was a new experience for her.

No one had ever included her in church activities in the four years since becoming a member of the congregation. Maybe it had more to do with a general fear of her husband than a desire to exclude her. But she'd still always longed to participate, to truly become a part of the church body. But she'd never been able or ready. Perhaps she was now.

She shifted the plate of homemade double chocolate brownies and picked up her pace as she spotted the bake sale table.

Audrey was already present, and waved her over. "Good morning." Audrey took the plate of goodies from Laurel's hands and found a vacant spot for it on the table. "Glad you could make it."

A cool, early spring gust stirred, making Laurel glad she'd thought to pull on a sweater before she left the house. "Thanks for inviting me." Laurel took the vendor apron Audrey handed over and tied it around her waist. A peek inside the pockets revealed a wad of bills and plenty of coins.

"It's long past time we got you involved." Audrey adjusted a few plates. "Especially now that Tommy's gone. I know how hard it probably was for you to even make it to church when he was alive."

If anyone other than Audrey had said such a thing, Laurel might have taken offense—not that it wasn't completely true. But Audrey knew firsthand what Laurel had lived with for so many years. Audrey had been Bobby's girlfriend before finally kicking him out of her house and her life. Then, of course, Bobby had found the Lord and changed.

Laurel suppressed a sigh. Maybe she should have tried kicking Tommy out. But no. She knew that wasn't the real catalyst that changed her brother-in-law's heart.

"Anyway," Audrey continued, "I'm hoping we'll see more of you around, especially at functions like this."

Laurel nodded. "Tommy would never have let me come. Not that he would have been at home with me. He'd have been out...doing whatever. But me...he'd have expected me to be waiting at home when he decided to show up."

Audrey stopped shuffling plates and turned to her. "I hope you know I would have reached out to you years ago, Laurel. But Tommy hated Bobby so much, and he hated me so much because of my connection to Bobby...I was afraid to make things worse for you."

Laurel glanced down and toyed with the hard, cold coins in her apron pocket. "I know. And you were right. It would have."

It might have made things worse for Audrey with

Bobby as well. If it hadn't been for Tommy's blind hatred of his brother, she and Audrey might have been friends. But then Audrey had extricated herself from the Kerr family, and their paths had stopped crossing, at least until Laurel started attending church. And her church attendance was such a sore spot with Tommy that Laurel didn't dare try to make friends while she was there.

Leftover loneliness brought the sting of tears. Laurel pulled them back with a deep breath as she turned from Audrey, casting her glance down the fairground midway in the hopes that her new friend wouldn't see.

Audrey's husband, Brent, led a small contingent of teenagers from church. All were either carrying or dragging coolers toward the bake sale.

"What's all this?" Audrey greeted him with a quick kiss before he situated the coolers beneath their tables.

"The guys here figured that if people might want a cookie, they might want a cold drink to go with it." Brent lifted a lid revealing soda cans and water bottles packed in ice.

"Good thinking, guys."

Brent fished a ten dollar bill from his pocket and bought cinnamon rolls for the boys with him, and one for himself, too. Then he smiled at Laurel. "Good morning."

"Good morning." She met his eyes briefly, then glanced away, hating that it still frightened her to connect with people.

"Where are your boys this morning?"

"They were still getting up and going when I left. They'll be along a little later with their grandmother."

"If they want to join us, they're welcome." Brent wiped icing from the corner of his mouth with a thumb. "The youth group will be selling hamburgers later to raise some money for summer camp."

"I'll tell them."

"Sorry I'm late." A new voice added to the mix, a voice she recognized and one that made her heart skip and her face flush in a new way.

Laurel turned to find Boyd's gaze fastened on her for a moment before he let it take in everyone else there. She'd never seen him looking so casual before. The jeans and short sleeved plaid shirt he wore untucked made him look less like a lofty doctor from an unreachable social sphere, and more like a regular guy who might, on occasion, get his hands dirty.

Audrey handed him a vendor apron. "Dr. Wendall, you didn't bring any goodies."

"I have a pretty poorly stocked pantry." He tied the apron around his waist.

"I guess you better get that taken care of before Wednesday then, seeing as our whole Sunday school class is coming to your house for dinner."

Boyd dismissed Audrey's concern with a wave of his hand. "No need. Y'all are bringing all the food. All I'm responsible for is the house to meet in."

Audrey shook her head as if he was pathetic, but she grinned. "Well, it better be very clean, then."

A line was forming for the cinnamon rolls and coffee cakes, so the conversation behind the table stopped as Laurel, Audrey, and Boyd turned to wait on customers. Traffic remained steady as the temperature warmed, and the next time she thought to glance at her watch, she was surprised to find a couple of hours had passed. Laurel shed her sweater and draped it over the back of a lawn chair.

"Hey." Boyd touched her arm. "Your cast is gone."

"Oh." Laurel rotated her wrist and the joint popped. "Yeah. A couple of weeks ago."

"Did everything heal OK?" He took her hand examined her wrist, feeling the bones and testing the range of motion. The touch was in no way inappropriate, but the gentleness of it made the breath in her lungs expand in such a way that it couldn't escape.

He glanced up expectantly, warm fingers still manipulating and massaging her hand.

"Um…yes." She prayed he couldn't see the heat rising from beneath her collar even though she could feel it creeping quickly into her cheeks. "Good as new."

"Good." He let her hand go, but didn't step away. "It's good to see you here, Laurel."

She smiled. "Thank you. It's good to be here."

He answered her smile with one of his own, the cleft in his chin deepening slightly as the corners of his eyes crinkled.

"Mom!" Joshua's voice rose above all the other fair noise in the background.

He and T.J. weaved a path through the thickening crowd to get to the bake sale table.

"Where's your grandma?"

"She's coming." T.J. answered. "She stopped at another booth down the road. She said she'd meet us here in a minute."

"Have you eaten?"

"Not since breakfast." Joshua examined the assortment of sweets laid out before him, eyeing the chocolate chip cookies in particular.

"Oh, no." She reached for her purse. "Go get a

hamburger first. Then come back here and pick something out for dessert."

"Tell you what." Boyd broke in, handing T.J. a fifty before Laurel could locate her wallet. "Go get yourselves a burger and bring one back for me and your mom and Miss Audrey, too. My treat."

T.J. and Joshua looked at each other, then they looked at her, waiting for permission.

She nodded. "Thank you, Boyd."

"My pleasure."

"Thank you," they both chorused. The boys wended their way from the table and down the midway until she lost sight of them. Then she glanced at Boyd who watched her as if he had something to say.

"Why don't you join us Wednesday at my house? Our class meets for a potluck meal once a month."

"But I don't attend your class."

"Well, maybe after you meet us for dinner, you'll decide to give it a try."

Laurel pretended to look for the boys even though she knew they'd be stuck in a line somewhere for a while. It seemed she'd gone from no social invitations ever to more than she knew what to do about. Maybe it was too soon to jump into a social circle. Maybe it would be inappropriate to blithely start meeting new people and making new friends a mere two months after her husband's funeral. She didn't know. What she did know, however, was that her heart leapt at the possibility.

"What should I bring?"

"Nothing." Boyd smiled. "Guests get to eat for free the first time. Just bring your lovely self, and we'll do the rest. OK?"

"OK." Still smiling like a silly girl, Laurel turned to greet the next customer.

Karen stood at the front of the line, glaring at her.

~*~

"Why was Grandma so mad?" Joshua dropped onto the couch as Laurel closed and locked the front door, then hung her purse on the rack.

She sighed heavily, trying to throw off the one unpleasant element in what had otherwise been the most pleasant day she'd had in a very long time. The reason for Karen's anger was no mystery, but how would the boys take the news that Dr. Wendall had invited her to his get together, and she had said yes? Their father's funeral had only been two months ago. Maybe it was too soon.

"Grandma was angry with me because she overheard Dr. Wendall invite me to dinner."

The boys stared for a moment, surprise raising their brows simultaneously.

"Like, on a date?" T.J. asked.

"No. Not like on a date. His Sunday school class has dinner together once a month, and he invited me to come along."

"Well, that sounds a little like a date," T.J. said.

"What did you say?" Joshua nearly jumped off the sofa.

Laurel didn't want to admit, even to herself, how much she looked forward to the dinner. She'd spent most of the day feeling young and hopeful—a nice change from tired and beat down. But she hadn't given much thought to how the boys might feel about it. The realization brought a measure of guilt with it. "I said yes. But if you boys don't like the idea, it's OK. I don't have to go."

"No!" They shouted nearly in unison.

"You should go," T.J. said. "It'll be good for you to have some friends."

An ache rose suddenly, and Laurel nodded. It would be good to have some friends if such a thing was even possible for her given her history in this town. She tamped the rising insecurity down. An invitation had been freely given, and she had accepted. A door had opened, and she'd agreed to walk through it. She would leave the rest to the Lord. "Well. You boys be thinking about what you want for supper. I'm going to take a quick shower."

Safely behind the closed bathroom door, Laurel glanced down at the hand Boyd had held when he'd noticed her cast was gone. His touch had been so warm and gentle that she almost couldn't comprehend it. She couldn't remember the last time Tommy had touched her so tenderly. Maybe he never had. And then the most wonderful man she'd ever known had invited her into his circle of friends, to share in an activity that bonded them all together. But she hadn't been able to relish the moment for long. The withering look Karen had given both of them ruined it and nearly drove her to withdraw her acceptance of his invitation. She removed the clip holding her hair and let the brazen mass tumble over her shoulders as she ran fingers through to loosen it.

The boys were supposed to have spent the night with their grandmother. But she'd been spitting mad by the time Laurel had arrived after the bake sale. The boys wouldn't have enjoyed their time there, and there was no telling what sorts of terrible things Karen would have said about her.

Then Karen had made a comment about Laurel rushing home to meet secretly with Boyd while her sons weren't home. She hadn't used the word whore, but the implication was unmistakable. That accusation had always been her mother-in-law's go-to fighting words. Since the day Tommy had brought her home to meet his mother, she'd been either using it outright to describe her, or implying it to keep her in her place.

T.J. and Joshua hadn't wanted to stay the night at that point.

Of course, Karen had turned on the tears and pleaded with her not to take the boys away, as if she'd never see them again.

The water was cold when she turned on the tap, so she let it run for a moment, opening the top drawer of the vanity for the toothpaste.

Tommy's razor lay beside the tube, and she lifted it to the light. Reminders of him were everywhere. On some level, she was reluctant to throw them out. They represented fifteen years of her life. She flattened her left hand and examined her wedding band.

Tommy hadn't wanted to get it for her. He had never worn one. He'd refused when she'd asked him to. He knew he was married and didn't need a ring to remind him.

She ran her thumb across the warm gold band. He had brought it to her during their first year together, after a particularly severe beating that had put her in bed for three days. He'd come home with this simple band. At the time, she thought he had meant to make up for the attack. But now she knew it had probably been his way of reminding her that she was married to him and couldn't leave.

She had received another beating a year or two later because he'd caught her not wearing it. She'd never taken it off again, and there had been so many times when she could feel the weight of it holding her down. Laurel slipped the ring off and examined it.

No beating would come tonight as a result of not wearing it. No beating would come ever again. She set the ring on the counter beside Tommy's razor, his toothbrush, his cologne, and shaving cream. Then she tested the temperature of the shower.

Tonight she would find a box and start gathering his things. He was gone...dead.

And she was no longer married. She was free, no matter what her mother-in-law thought about it.

~*~

Boyd rang Laurel's door bell, then took a step back and grasped her sweater in both hands.

The sound of high-spirited commotion inside drifted through the walls, then the door opened, revealing Joshua, whose face split into a grin. "Hi, Dr. Wendall."

"Hello, Joshua. Is your mom home?"

Laurel appeared behind her son, and the boy stepped aside.

"Boyd. Hi."

"Hi. You...um..." He couldn't speak.

Her cheeks and mouth were flushed a rosy pink and her dark hair fell unbound around her shoulders curling softly down her back. He'd never seen her with her hair loose. It made her look...different. "You left your sweater at the bake sale table."

"Oh." She took the sweater when he held it out.

"Thank you."

Joshua disappeared back into the house and the commotion began again.

Laurel stepped outside and closed the door. "Video games."

She wore a plain white t-shirt and faded jeans that fit in a way that made her appealing on a whole new level. Her feet were bare, toenails painted pink. And she smelled like a bouquet of fresh flowers.

A sudden gust caught one of her ebony curls and tossed it across her face.

On an impulse, Boyd reached out to move it. It felt as silky as it looked.

"Oh." Her eyes widened, then she apologized and gathered her hair into a ponytail, securing it with an elastic band she had around her wrist. Then she slipped the sweater on. "Do you want to sit for a minute?" She gestured to the steps leading up to the stoop. "I'd invite you in, but the boys have taken up the whole living room with their football game."

A loud cheer erupted inside.

"They take up a lot more space than they used to."

"I'd love to." He sat.

She joined him, sitting close enough that he could smell the clean fragrance of her perfume.

"Did you enjoy the bake sale today?" He asked the question more to have something to say than for information. She'd clearly enjoyed herself. In fact, he'd never seen her looking so at ease and happy.

She'd started out quiet in the way of a woman who was new in town, but had warmed up by the end of the afternoon.

"Yes." She leaned back against the porch railing and drew her knees up to her chest, wrapping arms around them, interlacing her fingers. "I've never been able to do anything like it before."

"Maybe you'll get to do a lot more of that kind of thing from now on."

She nodded and smiled.

Since he'd first really taken notice of Laurel Kerr, he had wondered if his attraction was genuine, or if it was simply misapplied compassion for a woman in a bad situation. But sitting here with her tonight, inhaling the fragrance of her perfume, stealing glances at her soft dark curls, fair skin, and earthy brown eyes, there was no doubt that his attraction to her was real and growing exponentially by the second.

A car crawled past in front of the house and Boyd dragged his gaze from her to watch it. He didn't recognize the driver or the passenger, but both craned their necks to get a look at who was sitting on Tommy Kerr's front porch with his wife.

Maybe he was rushing this. He glanced at Laurel who also watched the car with a furrowed brow. If word of his being here got back to her mother-in-law, it could make things difficult. Karen had very clearly not approved of Laurel's friendly interaction with him today at the bake sale.

Boyd was willing to allow that Karen's objection might not be to him personally. Maybe it was just too soon after her son's death. Maybe she wasn't yet ready to see her daughter-in-law enjoying herself in the company of others. Maybe she was simply the kind of woman who wanted those around her to be as mired in grief as she.

If that was the case, word of this—of him sitting here on Laurel's porch for the whole town to observe— might just bring the woman's wrath down harder on

Laurel.

As if she were thinking the same thing, Laurel looked down at her pink painted toes. The small sigh that slipped free seemed to suggest disappointment, but only for a moment. "Are you sure I don't need to bring anything to dinner on Wednesday?

"No." Boyd let a grin emerge. "No. If you decide you can stand us enough to come back next month, you can bring something then. Of course, if you decided to make a pan of those double chocolate brownies you brought to the bake sale today, I don't think anyone would complain. I know I wouldn't."

Soft brown eyes sparkled as she smiled, revealing a smooth line of white teeth which bore down on a smooth, full lip. Color rose to her cheeks, making him long to trace her cheekbone with the tips of his fingers...to urge her gently toward him...to taste a soft kiss...

She was so beautiful.

"Well..." He stood abruptly. "I should be going."

"Oh." She blinked, seeming surprised by his sudden movement. But she rose as well.

"I just came by to return your sweater."

"Thank you."

He ran a hand across the back of his neck and looked down, unable to meet her eyes. "I'll see you at church tomorrow."

"OK. And Wednesday, too. At six, right?"

He nodded lamely. "Right."

Laurel sounded so hopeful, so optimistically expectant.

As if it were contagious, that same optimism began to course through him as well. He met her gaze and, as another slow smile warmed her features, he was able to match it. This woman was worth pursuing. She may not be quite as ready to give her heart yet, but he would wait. He could demonstrate a different kind of love than she had ever known, and hopefully win her trust along the way.

8

It had been a long time since she had bothered with mascara. Laurel poked the wand into the tube she'd bought on her way home from work and twisted it closed, smiling at the frivolity. It had been an even longer time since she'd felt so young and lighthearted. Anticipation hadn't been a positive experience in at least fifteen years. But today...

All day she had felt nearly giddy with the anticipation of tonight's dinner at Boyd's. Now, she pressed a palm to her midsection as her heart fluttered around. She raised the same palm and smoothed it across her cheek, then she worked fingers through deep brunette curls and frowned.

Something about her hair bothered her. It had always possessed a wild quality that she'd never liked when she left it loose. It had been Tommy's favorite aspect of her appearance, but it had also worked against her so many times. An unwelcome memory assaulted her, of her husband's fingers buried in the unbound tangle of curls, not in a moment of tenderness or passion, but rather pulling, dragging her from one room to another as she begged him to stop.

But no...those memories had no place in her life anymore. She gathered the curls at her nape and twisted them up, securing it all with a clip and letting the ends fall where they would. Simple gold hoop earrings put the finishing touch on her appearance.

She took a step back from the mirror and gave a small twist setting the skirt of the green floral wrap dress into motion. The dress she'd pulled from the recesses of her closet hadn't been worn in so many years that it felt almost new. But she loved it. She'd always loved this dress. It made her feel pretty.

Laurel slipped on a pair of sandals and grabbed her sweater, just in case the evening air turned chilly. With a deep breath and a final glance in the mirror, she headed for the kitchen to put the finishing touches on dinner for the boys.

"Is that a new dress?"

Laurel set the dish of baked chicken on the stovetop and turned to find Joshua staring as if he wasn't sure who she was. She glanced down, and then turned the oven off. "No." She laid the pot holders aside and gave a pot of mashed potatoes a quick stir. "It's a very old dress."

"I've never seen you wear it."

"I probably haven't worn it since you were a baby." She resisted the impulse to ask how she looked. A twelve-year-old's opinion of her appearance probably would not do much to bolster her confidence.

T.J. joined them in the kitchen as Laurel was reaching into the cabinet for plates. "It's OK, Mom. We can handle dinner from here."

She turned to face the son who was as tall as she. "OK. You're sure you're OK with this...with me having dinner out tonight?"

"We're fine with it."

"It's not too soon?"

"For us, or for you?"

How could a fourteen-year-old possibly cut so precisely to the heart of the matter?

Laurel swallowed the sudden ache in her throat and looked down to cover the sting. It was too soon. Tommy had been gone two months. What would people think? What did her willingness to move on so quickly say about her? Would they all think that she was trying to force her way into a social circle in which she had no place and would never belong?

"It's OK, Mom," he said, as if he could detect her apprehension. "And you look good."

Laurel let a grin emerge. "Good, huh?"

"Yeah. Like a girl."

"What do I usually look like, if not a girl?"

T.J. shrugged. "I don't know. You look like a mom, I guess. Now, go." He took over transferring chicken and potatoes to plates and setting the table for two.

"You'll be OK here by yourselves?"

"Mom!"

She took a deep breath, nodded. Then she picked up the plate of double chocolate brownies she'd made and headed for the door.

Driving away from the confines of her shabby, older neighborhood, Laurel turned onto the highway that led to the subdivision where Boyd's house was located. The houses here weren't newer than hers, but they were much bigger and better maintained.

When she and Tommy had been dating, they would drive over and look at the stately homes with their green landscaped yards. Tommy would spew his hatred even then in the form of contempt filled comments about the neighborhood and its residents.

But Laurel thought the houses were beautiful—too good to be true.

Years had passed since she'd been on this side of town, yet she drove slowly down Boyd's street, admiring the houses anew, remembering clearly how she'd thought that life here must be ideal.

She came to Boyd's address and swallowed down the ache that rose with the realization that this was the house she had always most admired. It made her think of a Deep South plantation—even though she'd never seen one. She'd seen pictures, however, of lush homes with wide verandas and second story balconies; just like this house except perhaps larger in scale.

Tommy had once asked her which house she would live in if she could pick any one, and she'd chosen this very one. She turned into the semi-circular drive and parked behind another car, her heart hammering in her chest. This was Boyd's home, and she was about to go inside and see what she'd always thought of as her dream house. She squeezed her eyes shut and expelled an anxious breath. What had she been thinking, agreeing to this?

Shame stung. She knew exactly what she'd been thinking when she reached into her closet and pulled out her best dress. She'd wanted confirmation that she was still young and beautiful. And desirable. Laurel had wanted to believe that she had not wasted her best years, that life might still have something good in store, that a handsome, successful, kind hearted man could take an interest in her. But this was so far beyond her reach.

As nice as she knew everyone at church to be, she wasn't one of them. And, though they might politely tolerate her for one evening, there was no way they would ever be able to accept her as a part of their group. They were people with professional careers and stay at home moms who could afford to dote on their children and make beautiful homes for their families.

She didn't belong here. If she turned her car around and drove away, no one would miss her. They probably would not even notice she wasn't there. But Boyd would. And her not showing up without a good reason would hurt his feelings and possibly embarrass him in front of his friends. So, with a resigned sigh, she picked up the plate of brownies she'd made and stepped out of her car.

The stately white stone and columned porch of the two story house seemed as extravagant up close as it did from the street. Laurel's nerve held and she rang the bell.

Within a moment, Boyd opened the door, smiling warmly. "Hi, Laurel." The soothing tone of his voice lessened her apprehension.

But a sudden burst of laughter from inside the house reminded her that she had more than one person to impress tonight.

Boyd took the plate from her, pulling her focus back to him.

It was just dinner; just time spent with a man who had always treated her with kindness and consideration, who now seemed to notice her as a woman. The boys seemed to like him. There was nothing to fear. Only dinner with him and his friends. And if they were his friends, then they must be as nice as he was.

"Hi."

He wore khaki trousers and a yellow button down shirt, cuffs open and turned up a couple of times. The fact that he'd worked all day and stood here now, ready to go rather than sink into a battered old recliner in front of the television spoke of the professional and social chasm between them. What could he possibly see in her? She would be an idiot to imagine this dinner as anything other than a friendly invitation to join his Sunday school class.

"Come in."

A deep breath shored up her flagging self-image and at the same time heightened her awareness of him. The cologne he wore smelled spicy and clean, and probably expensive. She stepped across the threshold as he stepped aside to allow her entrance into the marble tiled foyer.

To the right was a formal living room, and to the left was a dining room. Directly ahead was a beautiful, wide staircase—absolutely worthy of a southern plantation.

Boyd turned and led her though the front hall beside the staircase, and into the heart of the house; the kitchen, which included a less formal eating space and a casual family room.

His other guests were congregated here, and their lively chatter stopped abruptly when she entered. But the conversation began again quickly enough after Audrey greeted her and introduced her to the class members present.

Some of them she knew. An odd wave of shame surfaced when she said hello to Justin Barnet. He was less intimidating dressed in jeans and a casual shirt, but his presence would only ever remind her of Tommy. And the Lord only knew what he must think of her.

He greeted her warmly, however, and introduced her to his wife Elaine.

But she knew Elaine, just as she knew Audrey, and Audrey's husband, Brent, and everyone else here who had grown up in this town as she had. She had been on the fringes of society then, and she felt ill at ease now, stepping away from the edge and closer toward the center of their society.

Boyd touched her elbow gently, guiding her to a stool at the counter in the midst of all of them, and Audrey placed a glass of iced tea in front of her.

A few minutes later, someone stepped inside from the back deck announcing that the steaks were ready— steaks, and she'd left her boys at home eating chicken and potatoes— and everyone else made their way outside carrying a dish of something—baked beans, potato salad, green beans—to place on the table.

The kitchen grew suddenly quiet.

"Time to eat." Boyd gave her a smile.

Laurel nodded, rose from her place and followed him outside.

~*~

The evening was cool, but not chilly.

Boyd bid goodbye to Brent and Audrey and returned quickly to the back.

Everyone was now gone except one.

Laurel wandered the perimeter of the deck, her wide, chocolate brown eyes taking in the sight of mid-spring blooms in flower beds. And as the evening turned dusky and the soft incandescent deck lighting warmed her skin, she turned to face him. "Do you do all this?" She swept a hand out, indicating the landscaping.

"I do some of it." He joined her in observing the view. "I hire a little help in the spring and summer. I'm not much of a gardener. But the beautiful yard came with the house. It seemed wrong to just let it go."

"It looks like a picture in a magazine...like it's ready for a photo shoot, but not like it's someplace that someone would actually live."

Boyd followed her gaze, trying to see the space from her perspective. It would be nice to spend more time out here doing something other than yard work. Maybe enjoying a cup of coffee in the cool of a summer morning, or a mug of hot cider in front of the stone fireplace on a crisp autumn evening; but with someone, not alone. Tonight, however, the yard did seem picture perfect. Maybe more so than usual with Laurel here in her emerald green dress, dark hair swept up accentuating the beautiful lines of her face.

Boyd turned back to close the lid on the grill and clean up a few more dishes.

She joined him in gathering dishes and platters, following him back into the kitchen to deposit them in the sink. She turned on the taps to start washing.

"Oh, no." Boyd turned them off again. "You're a dinner guest here. You're not allowed to wash dishes on your first visit."

"It'll just take a minute," she said softly. "And then it'll be done and you won't have to do it yourself. Let me help."

He relented, opening the dishwasher and pulling out the bottom rack to load the plates as she rinsed them off. This wasn't what he'd envisioned when he'd invited her here tonight, her standing at the kitchen sink cleaning up after everyone. But it did make a nice domestic picture of what life might be if he had someone to share it with. "So, has Blithe Settlement always been home for you?" A lame question and one he should already know the answer to.

"Yes. I've lived here since I was little."

"And your family—parents, brothers and sisters— do they still live around here?"

"No." She shrugged. "I don't think so."

He didn't know how to respond. Should he keep digging, or change the subject? He felt his brows draw together as he waited.

She handed him one plate after another.

He hoped she would offer more without him having to ask and potentially say something hurtful or offensive.

"I didn't know my father." She continued after a long moment. "And I was taken from my mother."

"Taken?"

"By the state. Child Protective Services took me from her when I was seven."

"I'm sorry." He pushed in the lower rack as she finished the last of the plates and began rinsing the tea glasses. "Was it very traumatic?"

"You mean did they rip me from her arms as she pleaded with them not to take me?" She glanced at him and grinned softly. "No. She wasn't even home. The social worker came to the door with a warrant and a police officer, helped me pack a suitcase, and took me away. After that I lived in foster homes."

"You never saw your mother again?"

"Not that I'm aware of. I'm not sure I would recognize her if I passed her on the street. As for brothers or sisters..." Laurel shrugged. "There were none at the time. But I guess there could be some now that I never knew about."

"What was your experience in foster care like?"

"It wasn't terrible. It was never stable, though. Every couple of years I'd get sent to a new home. The families were always nice enough. Nothing bad ever happened to me. But the homes weren't mine, and that was always pretty clear. I just wanted a home that was my own, and, as I got older, some kids that I could love and take good care of. I guess I just wanted a family." Her gaze fell to the now empty sink for a moment. "I guess, when I met Tommy, I saw him as my way out. I knew what kind of family he came from. I'd experienced his temper firsthand before we ever got married. I guess I just never thought about how it might affect any kids we had. It was stupid of me."

Boyd stood silently, drying the counter with a dishtowel, waiting to let her say whatever she wanted, sensing that if he'd just be patient, she might open up more.

She turned the taps off and let her gaze travel to the window and out to the backyard she had so admired. "I thought he would change." She admitted softly. "Right up to the very end, I hoped he would somehow change...that God would change his heart."

"Maybe he did." Boyd kept his tone even. "I didn't have a chance to tell you before. He looked me in the eye and said one word before...before...the paramedics took over." Boyd paused. "Forgive. He said 'forgive.' Nothing more."

"Forgive whom?" She looked at him in wonder.

"I don't know. Himself, you, me...or God." Boyd took a deep breath. "We'll never know."

She fell silent for a long moment, lost in thought and what seemed like regret. Finally, she smiled and seemed to switch gears. "What about your family. Where are they?"

Boyd closed the dishwasher and turned to lean against the counter behind him. This line of conversation was sure to lead them right back to the same place as when they'd spent their lunch hour together at the deli. He didn't want to talk about it—all the events that had led to his move here. But unless she went home tonight and he never saw her again, he'd end up needing—maybe even wanting—to tell her eventually. Why not now? What was there to lose at this point?

"Back in Houston." He let his gaze skim the lush, green lawn outside.

"Oh," she said softly.

For a long moment, the only sound was a pair of mockingbirds in a nearby tree outside. Then a gentle breeze stirred, setting a deeply toned wind chime in motion.

"It's OK," she finally offered. "If you don't want to talk about it—whatever happened in Houston. Probably no one will understand as well as I do experiencing something you don't want to tell anyone about."

He nodded his gratitude for her perceptiveness as well as her refusal to push him to tell the story. But he wanted to tell her, at least as much as he could want to tell anybody. "I was sued for malpractice."

Her delicate, dark brows drew together. "What?"

"I had been practicing with the group in Houston for about a year." Boyd turned back to face her. "I was fresh out of my residency, just starting out, and I saw a patient for the other internist in the group while he was on vacation. My colleague had been treating this patient for…well…several issues. But I thought the symptoms he presented with on that day warranted more tests, so I ordered them. Then I passed the information to the patient's regular physician.

"My colleague evidently didn't follow up with the

patient, and the patient died two weeks later. If the findings from the tests that I ordered had been addressed, he might have made it. His family named my colleague and me in the malpractice suit."

Laurel's brow creased further and she shook her head slightly. "I don't understand. If you weren't his regular doctor, and you were just filling in for his regular doctor, why did they sue you? You're the one who ordered the tests that might have saved his life."

Boyd drew in a breath and reached deep down to the place inside where he did feel some understanding for the family who had accused him. "I couldn't say why. Maybe they thought it might somehow right a wrong, or fill a void."

"So, what happened?"

"My insurance company decided to settle. The doctors in the group thought it would be best for everyone if my colleague and I left the practice. He retired. I came here."

"So, you left your whole life in Houston—your family—and you came here where you didn't know anyone."

He nodded. "I had a big, new house. I had to sell it. My fiancée broke off our engagement..." He let his voice trail off. What else was there to say about it? His whole world had fallen apart. His dreams shattered.

"Boyd, I'm sorry." Her quiet, heartfelt sympathy made him feel so small; petty, even.

"Well, now you know." He tossed the dishtowel to the counter and forced a smile. "I'm not the respectable doctor everyone here seems to think I am."

"Of course you are."

"And I know what I've gone through pales in comparison to the trials you've had to face."

"Trials of my own making, mostly." She crossed to the deck's door and gazed outside. "But you were accused for no reason."

Boyd shook his head and followed her. "No. I should have followed up with the patient. I was responsible. When I saw him in the exam room it became my responsibility. I was young and inexperienced. And busy with other things. It was my mistake." Boyd opened the door and stepped outside to straighten the table and chairs.

The evening was growing dusky and the spring breeze cooled.

Laurel folded her arms and wrapped them around herself as she stepped out after him.

"It's getting cool. Would you like to go back inside? Or I could get a fire going in the hearth, if you'd like and we could sit out here."

"A fire would be nice."

The breeze toyed with a few fallen tendrils of her hair as it raised a charming pink flush to her cheeks, and her expression conveyed such admiration that, in this moment, he would have done anything to please her.

A fire *would* be nice. But her smile—it didn't judge or condemn, it let his past go and encouraged him to do the same. Her smile was even nicer.

~*~

Boyd settled her into the dark wicker sofa across from the hearth and got a small fire going. Then he stepped back inside for a moment, returning with a light blanket for her, a bag of marshmallows, and a skewer.

He opened the blanket and spread it over her, letting her arrange it suitably. She used the small bit of action as an excuse to glance down until she was certain the prickle of tears wouldn't swell into actual drops. A deep breath reined the emotion in before Boyd could see it and ask what was wrong.

Nothing was wrong. But how could she explain that no man had ever treated her with such care and consideration? She could not admit such a thing to him. Neither could she admit that, in doing so, he made her feel as if she was worthy of his consideration...of being treated like a lady. The small gesture may not have meant anything to him. He might treat any guest in his home the same way. But it made her feel as if he saw her as more than just the cashier at the grocery store, or the widow of the town drunk, and it touched her heart.

Boyd sat on the edge of the stone hearth and pierced a marshmallow.

The fluffy white treat, held near the flame, slowly toasted until it just began to blister.

When Boyd took it from the fire and offered it to her, she pulled it gently from the skewer.

"You said you had a fiancée in Houston."

Boyd nodded and poked another marshmallow into the heat, but didn't look at her.

"What was she like?"

He remained silent for a long moment.

Laurel enjoyed the warm sweetness of the toasted marshmallow as she tried to imagine the woman Boyd would choose for a wife.

She'd probably be tall and willowy and graceful, with long, straight blonde hair and big blue eyes. Her wardrobe would be impeccable, composed of expensive clothes and accessories. Her makeup would be flawless although she would be just as beautiful without it. Laurel pictured her meeting friends at an expensive restaurant for lunch—the kind of place where the table would be covered with a cloth and have a vase of fresh flowers.

"She was an interior designer." Boyd took another marshmallow from the fire and offered it to her. Warm and gooey and soft, it stuck to her fingers as she pulled it from the skewer.

The image of a woman of leisure, destined to be a doctor's wife, vanished like mist only to be replaced by an image of the same beautiful blonde, clad in a tailored suit and expensive shoes, sitting behind a fancy desk and poring over fabric swatches while she made important phone calls.

"Was she good at it?"

Boyd sort of half nodded, half shrugged. "I guess. I let her decorate my house. I figured it was going to be our house, so she'd end up decorating it anyway. She did a good job. It was a little too formal for me, but I didn't think it was worth arguing about. It made her happy."

He offered her another toasted marshmallow and she took it.

Tommy never argued either, but not because he was a tolerant, peace-loving man, or concerned in any way about her happiness. He skipped the disagreement altogether and went straight to violence.

A man who would let a woman be herself, and choose his battles carefully, not arguing or attacking over things that really didn't matter, would be a blessing that Laurel almost couldn't fathom. His fiancée must have been an exceptionally foolish woman.

"And she broke the engagement because of the lawsuit?"

The marshmallow he held to the flame caught fire and he pulled it out and blew on it. He pulled the charred remains from the skewer and popped the oozing black and white mess into his mouth. He nodded. "I think so. I mean, she didn't put it quite that way. But if the lawsuit had never happened, we'd probably be married today. When I left my place at the group practice, I couldn't keep the big house in the posh neighborhood. I wanted to leave Houston and make a fresh start somewhere else. She made it pretty clear she did not want to leave Houston..." his voice trailed off, and then he rose from the hearth and came to sit beside her on the thickly cushioned sofa.

"I'm sorry," Laurel said.

"Well," Boyd drawled the word. "It was a hard thing. But now I thank God for it."

"Why?"

"Better for it to happen before the wedding than after. That sounds trite, I know. And I didn't appreciate it when people said it to me at the time. But they were right." He stretched an arm across the back of the sofa behind her and she could feel his warmth. "And looking back, I'm not sure it would have been a good marriage. I can recognize qualities about her now that may not have been quite so easy to overlook after a few years of marriage. And I'm sure by now she's probably made the same realization about me."

"Do you ever hear from her?"

"Every once in a while she calls."

A cool gust set the wind chimes in motion again and whipped a stray tendril across her face.

Boyd brushed it back again with gentle fingertips.

The sensation made her breath catch and she had to look away from him for a moment. "So, how did you get *here*? I don't imagine there are many people in Houston who've ever heard of Blithe Settlement."

"When everything blew up, I went to talk to an advisor I'd had in med school." Boyd's gaze meandered across the darkening yard. "He had been a mentor to me during school and my residency. He knew Dr. Moore. Do you remember him?"

Laurel smiled and nodded. "He was my doctor growing up, and he was the boys' doctor when they were babies, until you came."

"He was getting ready to retire, and looking for someone to take over his practice. Even after everything that happened, my advisor was willing to give me a good reference. And I thought Blithe Settlement sounded like a peaceful place."

Laurel felt her brows rise at the irony.

"You don't agree?" He asked with a grin.

"Blithe Settlement has been many things, in my experience. But peaceful has never been one of them. At least, not until recently."

His smile faded, but didn't disappear completely. "Seems like that's true for a lot of people here. I guess that's true for people everywhere. I'm just better acquainted with a wider variety of people here than I was back in Houston."

She nodded, and then looked out over the yard.

Darkness had fallen, but the flower beds were illuminated by solar powered lanterns, and the details of the stone patio were visible in the warm glow of the fire.

She leaned back into the sofa cushions and drew

her feet underneath her. "This really is picture perfect, Boyd. I've never seen a more beautiful place. My backyard is a mess of mud puddles, trampled grass, and old toys."

"There's beauty in that, too." He stretched his other arm across the back of the sofa and gazed intently into the flames.

Laurel glanced away from the broad expanse of his chest and pulled the blanket a little closer.

"You should have seen me trying to take care of this yard the first spring and summer I was here."

She grinned and met his gaze.

"I'd never done yard work beyond mowing the lawn as a kid. And I'd spent the last decade in school, and then trying to get my career started. Then I ended up with this place, and this yard, and I was dumb enough to think I could manage it myself in addition to trying to get a new practice established.

"The house had been vacant for about a year, and the water had been turned off, so the sprinkler system hadn't been running. Half the lawn had died. Completely. And I thought digging up the dead turf and laying down new sod would be an easy Saturday project."

Laurel smiled, knowing from experience what came next; picturing the refined doctor from the big city out in the yard dirty and sweaty. "Let me guess. You were a little sore the next day."

"Yes," he said. "A little sore. In the same way that an ostrich is a little bird, or Mount Rushmore is a little statue…"

Her grin spread into a full smile, and then a laugh broke free.

"…or the Grand Canyon is just a little stream in

the desert. Yes, I was a little sore. I felt a little soreness in muscles I didn't even know existed. And I'm a doctor, so I know about pretty much all of them. And you're laughing at me."

She was laughing, and he didn't seem to mind despite his playful accusation. So she let the laughter come, allowing his smile to warm her heart.

He raised a hand and caressed her cheek, making the breath catch in her chest.

"I've never seen you laugh before." His gaze took in the whole landscape of her face. "You have the most beautiful smile I've ever seen. And I'd really like to tell you just how long I've admired you, but I'm a little ashamed to admit it. And I'm so very sorry if my admiration ever caused any trouble for you...with Tommy."

She shook her head. "You never—"

"I did." He laid a warm hand, gentle on her shoulder.

"No." She stopped him before he could go further. "No matter what you did or said, or thought you did or said...nothing Tommy ever did was because of you. Your kindness has always meant so much to me. It proved to me at some of the worst times in my life that there were good men, compassionate men. It made me hope that men like you were maybe the rule, and men like Tommy were the exception. And it gave me a goal to aim for in raising my boys.

"I never dared to hope they'd grow up to be doctors or anything like that. I'd never be able to give them the advantages they'd need to achieve something so wonderful. But that they might work hard and be successful at something..." Laurel let her voice trail off when she saw traces of mist cloud his eyes.

He glanced away and cleared his throat, seeming to rein in the sudden emotion.

"What?" She touched his knee lightly.

"I've felt like such a failure—for years. Since the lawsuit. There's been nothing I could do to regain the ground I'd lost or to repair the damage. I never would have imagined that someone was looking at me and seeing...success."

He felt like a failure? All she could see when she looked at him was a man who had achieved more success than anyone in her life ever had—herself included. How could he perceive himself as a failure?

"Well, you might not have a prestigious medical practice in Houston. But I know how much the folks in this town love and appreciate everything you do for them. You go above and beyond in a way that I expect big city doctors probably don't. And this may not be as big or as fancy a house as you had back then, but I think it's the best one in the whole town, and this is the most beautiful backyard I've ever had the pleasure of sitting in. And you may not have the beautiful, successful fiancée of your dreams, but like you said, maybe she wasn't the one for you." Laurel was just about to shrug and say something lame, like *you never know*. But before she could, he leaned close and pressed a soft kiss to her lips.

Surprise quickly gave way to consent, and she let her eyelids drift closed, savoring the softness of his mouth, the trace of sweetness leftover from the marshmallows they'd eaten, and the warmth of his arms as he drew her gently closer, enfolding her in a way she'd never experienced before; not forceful and demanding, but rather generous and protective. His arms were strong and able to bring her completely to him, but instead he let her come to him, on her own terms, in her own time. Slowly, she did.

Cool evening air nipped at her cheeks despite the fire glowing only a few feet away.

Boyd's hands caressed her face, then her shoulders and bare arms, making her draw closer still because she'd never felt so cherished and wanted. And this man...though she'd been acquainted with him for years, she barely knew him, really. But she knew him well enough to know that, if he chose her, he would never betray her. He'd never hurt her intentionally. She could trust him. And she could love him.

He seemed to read her mind somehow, to know that she wanted him to kiss her even more deeply, to show her exactly how desirable he found her, that she was still worth wanting. He seemed to know, but he couldn't possibly.

And this evening—this most perfect evening, in this most beautiful place—felt like a beginning. Like a fresh start. A promise for the future whispered through her heart as Boyd's arms enveloped her, as she heard the sounds of the coming night and the crackling fire.

Then she heard something else; something more familiar. Laurel pulled her mouth from his and pushed out of his embrace, searching his face as tears stung suddenly.

She heard Tommy's voice in her memory, and he was calling her a whore.

9

"Laurel, what is it?" Boyd reached out for her as she backed out of his arms and away from him.

She looked stricken. She shook her head and raised a hand to cover her mouth as tears filled her eyes.

"I'm sorry." He apologized, but she had kissed him back, he was certain. There had been no hesitation, no protest. He had not coerced her or applied any pressure. Had he?

"No." Her response came out in a breathy whisper. "Don't apologize. This is my fault. I shouldn't be here."

"What do you mean?" He leaned in closer, but she countered by getting up and putting the sofa between them. He rose and faced her, trying to shake the sudden confusion from his mind.

"He was right." Laurel took a deep breath and seemed to quell the tears. But what she said still made no sense. "He must have seen, must have sensed something."

"He must have sensed what? Who?"

"Tommy...he must have known I had these feelings."

"What feelings?"

"This." She spread her arms, palms up, as if to clarify.

But he still didn't understand.

"I think I always wanted this...always wanted you. I would tell myself that all I really wanted was a man who would treat me with kindness and consideration; a man who would speak respectfully to me, the way you always have. I would tell myself that all I wanted was for Tommy to treat me that way. I prayed for God to change his heart. But that wasn't what I really wanted. It was you."

Maybe what she was saying shouldn't please him the way that it did. He had wrestled mightily with his feelings for her. But now he knew he wasn't alone. His affection had not been unrequited.

"I had no right." Her voice was barely audible.

"Laurel, if you've had feelings for me, I never knew it. I could never tell." He came around the sofa to close the distance between them. "And if I couldn't tell, no one else could either. You never acted in any way inappropriately."

"But my feelings were inappropriate, and they were more than a longing to be treated better. They made me wish I had never married him...that if I had just been more content and not so desperate to escape the life I'd had...if I had just waited and never married him, then I would have been free...and he knew it. He saw it. And he was right.

"No, I never *did* anything I shouldn't have or that could be misconstrued. But in my heart..." Her voice trailed off, and she pressed a hand to her chest. Then she shook her head as if to say she couldn't continue, and she turned to face the yard she had admired only a few moments ago.

But he would not let this go. He would not let guilt for a sin not committed come between them before they even had a chance to begin. So they had both wrestled with feelings. Feelings were hard to control. And neither had acted on those feelings. Neither of them had done anything wrong. And from what she was saying, she'd not really realized she had the feelings until now.

He strode across the patio to where she stood. He would convince her. She was free now to love whomever she chose and to act on any feelings she might have for him. She was no longer tied to a man who would terrorize her and make her life a misery.

He reached for her elbow, to turn her to face him, and she recoiled defensively, as if she was preparing for an assault.

Immediately, Boyd withdrew. He was an idiot for forgetting.

For an instant, her expression betrayed fear and an expectation of violence. Then it faded to regret, and she reached out to him. "I'm sorry."

He took the hand she offered and raised it to his mouth, pressing a kiss to the back. Then he gently urged her into an embrace, and she pressed her forehead to his shoulder and allowed him to hold her. Tears would not have surprised him, in fact, he expected them.

But she shed none. She simply stood within the circle of his arms, leaning on him, her hands clutching the fabric of his shirt.

He was at a total loss as to how he ought to react. What should he do now? What did she expect? What did she need?

The very last thing he wanted was to rush or push or demand anything from her. The Lord knew she'd had enough of that in her lifetime. So he stroked her back and let her be, listening to the rhythm of her breathing, and feeling her soft curls tickling his face. On an impulse, he pressed a kiss to the top of her head. That seemed to bring her back around.

"What do you want from me, Boyd?"

The whispered question surprised him.

"I don't want anything from you." He drew back, and she looked into his eyes. "I just want to know you."

"What do you suppose I could possibly have to offer? I'm a grocery store cashier. I live in an old, eleven hundred square foot house down by the railroad tracks. I have two children—one's a teenager, and the other will be soon. You said you've admired me for a long time, but why on earth would you? I'm...nobody."

Boyd shook his head and pressed a palm to her cheek. "You're not nobody, Laurel. There's a goodness in you, despite everything you've been through. You've got the most gentle, open heart I've ever seen. I don't understand how you're not bitter or mistrustful of everyone...and how you see the best in people. You seem to see me in a completely different light than I do, and it makes me think that maybe it's time to stop feeling sorry for myself."

She glanced down, and although he wanted to tip her chin up so she'd look at him, he would never again insist in such a way. Not with her. So he touched her hair, working one curl around a finger. "Just tonight you've made me see this place from a different perspective. You see incredible beauty and blessing here. I've always seen this place—this house and my practice—as the life I had to settle for. And to top it all off, you are the most beautiful woman I've ever seen. So, there's that, too."

As he hoped, she smiled. But the moment was brief, and she withdrew again into her troubled thoughts with a slight shake of her head.

"I feel as if we've been through a lot together in the past few months. Even though we didn't technically go through it *together*, I couldn't help but feel involved. I hope we get to go through a lot more together. Better times, I hope. And I'm a patient man, so I can wait if you need time until you feel more ready...until Tommy's memory is not so persuasive. I can wait, as long as you assure me now that I can see you again soon. That you want to see me again. That you won't leave here tonight, and then tomorrow be back to calling me 'Dr. Wendall' again, and me just seeing you around town like I would anyone else."

She searched his face for a moment, then shook her head. "I can't see that happening."

"Good." He pressed a kiss to her forehead and her eyelids drifted closed.

Her hand felt soft and small when he took it and gently led her back to the wicker sofa in front of the fireplace.

They sat, and she pulled the blanket over her legs. Then she laid her head on his shoulder and intertwined her long, slender fingers with his.

If she wanted to talk, he'd talk. If she simply wanted to sit and gaze into the fire, he'd do that. But he would do everything he could to keep her from going home tonight with thoughts of Tommy Kerr foremost in her mind.

~*~

Karen's car was parked on the curb when Laurel

pulled her car into the driveway.

Laurel couldn't stifle the burdened sigh that slipped out, or the overwhelming sense of dejection that settled into her heart. This evening had hit a bumpy patch, no doubt about it. But it had ended well. In fact, she would call it wonderful despite the bumps. But she was a fool to think she'd ever really be free.

Karen had overheard Boyd's dinner invitation. It didn't matter that it was a dinner party rather than a date, and that there were several people involved, not only Boyd. No doubt, her mother-in-law was waiting inside now hoping Laurel would stay out all night because nothing would bring her more pleasure than proof that Laurel really was the whore she'd always thought she was. The fact that she was home well before the boys' bedtime would make up for nothing.

But...Laurel sighed...she couldn't stay out here all night waiting for Karen to leave. And she was probably peeking out the window right now to see what she would do. So Laurel pulled keys from the ignition and stepped out of the car. The door was unlocked, so she opened it and slipped into the living room.

The boys were playing video games.

Karen was sitting in Tommy's chair, scowling.

"Hey, Mom." Joshua put his game controller away and rose from the floor.

T.J. did the same.

"Did you boys get your homework done?"

"Yes, ma'am."

The boys cleared snack dishes from end tables and took them to the kitchen. But neither asked how the dinner had gone. Most likely, they simply knew better than to bring it up in front of their grandmother. They made a last, brief appearance in the living room to kiss her goodnight, and then they disappeared into their rooms.

Laurel met Karen's condemning stare for a moment, and then turned for the kitchen where she could, hopefully, busy herself tidying up. Thankfully, a few dishes waited in the sink. The counters could use a wipe down as well.

But Karen followed right behind, undeterred. "Did you have a nice time?" The question came out sounding like a hiss, and was clearly intended to accuse her of something sinful.

Laurel washed the dishes, set them in the rack, and tried to formulate a response that would not set her mother-in-law off.

She might say, yes, she'd had a very nice time. Spending time in the company of a man who truly saw her as a person with feelings, worthy to be treated with care and respect had refreshed her in a way she couldn't describe. A smile tried to rise as she recalled the way his kiss had caught her off guard. Seeming to spring from some innate tenderness inside of him, it had been unplanned and not intended to manipulate her in any way. So very different than any other experience she'd ever had.

But she might also say no. Tommy's memory still carried so much influence, and his false accusations still hounded her to such a degree that the most honest, tender moment of the evening had been irreparably spoiled. The memory of that first kiss would forever be marred by the sound of Tommy's voice in her head.

Either way, Karen could not be mollified. She would never accept Laurel's ability to move past Tommy's death, which was ironic given the fact that

Karen had never approved of her daughter-in-law.

"What brings you to the house tonight, Karen?" Laurel wiped down the counters and rinsed the dishrag. "It's not like you to come here."

"I just wanted to make sure the boys were all right, seeing as you went off with a man and left them alone."

"They're old enough to stay alone for a couple of hours. And I wasn't just off with some man. I was at a dinner party at Boyd Wendall's house with his whole Sunday school class."

"What business do you have being out at all? Tommy's barely been gone two months."

Laurel found it almost amusing when Karen made her accusations in a hissing whisper, as if she didn't want the boys to overhear the fight. As if they didn't know just how far from ideal their family life had been. "Yes, but he *is* gone. And he wasn't a very good husband to me while he was here. Nor was a he a good father. And who I choose to spend time with now doesn't concern you."

"It does concern me. As the grandmother of those two boys it concerns me very much."

"Well, as the mother of those two boys, I'd say it concerns me and them and no one else."

"Some *mother* you are, running around before your murdered husband's grave has even settled...acting like a—"

"Do not call me a whore." Laurel was surprised by the steel in her own voice. "If you ever call me that again, you will not be welcome in this house. I was never anything but faithful to Tommy. But he, on the other hand, cheated on me for the entire fifteen years of our marriage with a string of different women.

Including the one he was with on the night he was shot."

"And isn't it convenient that your Dr. Wendall happened to be there the night he was shot."

"What does that have to do with anything?"

"It seems a little suspicious to me that the man you're running around with now was there at the scene that night to make sure your husband didn't survive."

Laurel shook her head and tried to make sense of what Karen was saying. "What are you talking about?"

"You know full well what I'm talking about." Karen stepped closer, causing Laurel to step back. "He's a doctor. Don't you know he could have saved Tommy if he'd wanted to? But he didn't want to because he wanted you. And you wanted him."

"Boyd is a doctor." Laurel's breath nearly failed her in the face of Karen's reasoning. "But he's not God. There wasn't much he could do right there in the parking lot for three gunshot wounds to the chest."

"Oh, yes there was." Karen's volume had risen. She was so convicted of her own righteousness, she'd forgotten all about keeping the ugly truth from her grandsons. "He could have saved Tommy. If he'd wanted to."

"If he could have saved Tommy, he would have."

"And I see how you take his side now." Karen's tears started. "It wouldn't surprise me if the two of you had it all planned."

There was no way to hide the rising shock. A glance down the hallway confirmed Laurel's suspicion that the boys were out of bed and listening to every word their grandmother was saying.

"So...you think Boyd and I planned it."

"It wouldn't surprise me."

"You think we could have planned for him to go to a bar and get drunk, and then pick up a woman there in the presence of that woman's husband. We planned that, Boyd and I? That's what you're saying."

As absurd as it sounded, Karen didn't back down.

"We planned for him to take her to the quick stop for additional liquor and condoms—because that's what he bought while he was in there. Did you know that? And we planned for her husband to follow them. And shoot Tommy three times."

Karen held her ridiculous ground with a defiant stare.

"You have lost your mind."

"How dare you say such a thing to me!"

"No one planned what happened to Tommy. It was only a matter of time before his own bad behavior caught up with him. The truth is that the plan I *was* making involved leaving him and possibly moving to Alaska."

Karen gasped as if Laurel had just delivered a blow. "You would leave your husband? You would take his children away from him?"

"It's doesn't really matter now, does it?"

Karen raised a hand to her mouth and pooled tears spilled over as if her heart had shattered.

Laurel paused and sighed. To experience the death of a child was unfathomable to her, so she could hardly understand what her mother-in-law was going through. True, Tommy had been her husband. But she was convinced that the emotions governing her reaction to his death were anything but typical. Grief was present in her heart, but only in as much as she grieved for Tommy's wasted life. And unless he was asking for God's forgiveness, she grieved for his lost soul. Beyond that, there was only relief.

But Karen had lost her son. She'd lost both sons, really. Bobby had left a few years ago and rarely came home. And now Tommy was dead. That left Karen with two daughters, one of whom left town years before Bobby and, as far as Laurel knew, hadn't spoken to her mother since. The other was in prison. Laurel and the boys were all Karen had left.

Laurel turned with an apology in mind, but Karen spoke before she could.

"You are a cold-hearted one, Laurel." Karen had recovered. Her eyes were dry, if red rimmed, and her lips pursed into a tight, thin line before she continued. "I regret that you ever married Tommy. If you had been a better wife, he would have been a better man."

Laurel's apology died before it had the chance to be spoken. Her mother-in-law's disapproval didn't even sting anymore. But the time spent with Boyd this evening seemed to have empowered her. Not only did the barb not sting, it didn't intimidate her either. "The only thing I regret is not leaving years ago."

The expression on Karen's face morphed before Laurel's eyes. Where there had been grief and hurt, suddenly there was anger, and then rage. Karen turned, retrieved her purse from the living room, and slipped out the front door so calmly and quietly that Laurel couldn't quell the rising sense that she stood in the eye of a storm that would soon get a whole lot worse.

~*~

Boyd finished cleaning the kitchen and dropped

into the dark leather of the sofa. He reached for the remote, intending to watch a little news before he turned in. But his gaze landed on the phone beside it.

Laurel had left only a half hour ago, and it would probably be more appropriate to wait, but he wanted to call now. The evening felt unfinished, and he worried about the second thoughts she might be having about him now. He wanted to call, but now was probably not the time. So he left the phone where it was, pointed the remote at the large flat screen, and turned it on.

An attractive news anchor reviewed the day's events, but Boyd's mind wandered back to the evening, especially the part spent alone with Laurel. He replayed the part of the conversation when she'd asked what he wanted from her, as if she had nothing of value to offer...as if he were somehow above her station in life. Or maybe the question had an even worse implication. Maybe her life had so accustomed her to being used and manipulated that she couldn't believe any man would want to spend time with her simply because she was so...what? What was she? What was it about her that made him simply want to be in the same place with her...to want to know every detail about her?

Maybe it was only that she saw things so differently than he did. She had managed to make him see this place through new eyes and from a new perspective. No longer did his life here seem like the backup plan, or simply the place he landed when he fell and from which he couldn't pull himself back up. Now he looked around and saw God's abundant provision.

His life in Houston had fallen apart, and he'd

spent the years since feeling as if he was living amidst the shattered pieces. But that wasn't true at all. He had built a new life here—a real life, and although it was lonely at times, it was no less worth living.

"'For I know the plans I have for you,' declares the Lord...'" Words from the television penetrated his thoughts and snapped his focus back to the screen. A commercial played for a large Austin area church, featuring a popular pastor. The man preached to a congregation of thousands every week, yet now as he looked into the lens of the camera, Boyd felt as if the man's message spoke to him in particular. "...'plans to prosper you and not to harm you, plans to give you hope and a future...' The Lord hasn't forgotten about you. He sees you and He loves you. And, while the plan may not look like you imagined it would, it has always been the right plan."

The commercial ended with phone numbers, website addresses, and worship times. But Boyd paid no attention. He was struck suddenly by the idea that this had been God's plan all along—that God had intended for him to end up here.

Was it possible that God had used the lawsuit to turn his head and his heart away from the excessive, pride-filled life he had been embarking upon? Had the lawsuit itself been part of the plan? Boyd had certainly been humbled by it. It had had a refining effect, making him a more careful physician and a more patient man.

He had reached a point of contentment with what he had now in terms of possessions. But what did that say about him when only a couple of hours ago Laurel had sat on his back patio telling him this was the most beautiful place she'd seen? He had spent all these years seeing this place as a step down.

Shame rose from the core of his soul at the level of pride he'd allowed himself to feel—had considered himself justified in feeling. That shame drove him directly to repentance on his knees beside the leather sofa he'd spent thousands on at his fiancée's request.

He had wasted years telling himself that this was where God had placed him and he would abide—until the Lord restored him to his rightful position. But why couldn't this be his rightful position and the place God intended for him all along—as a family doctor in Blithe Settlement, Texas?

And now that he had connected with Laurel, he could see how life here could be so sweet. It could be better by far than anything his life in Houston might have ever had to offer.

And it seemed the Lord was willing to give it to him despite his arrogance, pride, and self-pity.

10

Laurel spooned the remainder of the leftover mashed potatoes into a storage container destined for the refrigerator. She accepted a kiss on the cheek from each of her sons as they brought their dishes from the table to the sink.

"Thanks for lunch, Mom." T.J. turned back to clear a few more dishes. "Can Joshua and I play video games?"

She nodded and rinsed the plates as the boys escaped to the living room. The sound of another chair scraping the floor as it pushed back from the table stopped her heart.

Boyd accepted her dinner invitation after church and had joined them for their Sunday meal. But for a moment, time seemed to rewind itself and Tommy was there, sitting at the table, pushing his chair back after finishing another beer. Now his footsteps crossed the floor toward her, and her every muscle tensed with expectation. If he was coming to her it would either be to bully her outright for some reason she couldn't see, or to make a sexual demand.

He set his plate on the counter, then turned and leaned back against it beside her, and suddenly he was Boyd again. There was no threat, no impending violence.

Laurel took a deep breath and let it out, expelling the unwarranted tension with it.

He laid a hand on her arm, then leaned over and pressed a soft kiss to her cheek. "Thanks for lunch."

She smiled. "You're welcome. Do you want to go play video games too?"

"Maybe later." He grabbed a dishtowel and dried the dishes as she finished washing. "You OK?"

"Yes." She nodded. "Sometimes it just seems as if he's still here. I'll hear a neighbor's truck drive past, and my heart will start pounding. Just now, the way the chair sounded on the floor when you got up from the table...I don't know. Something about the sound reminded me of him, and I felt as if he was here...."

Boyd gently stacked the dried dishes, listening.

"Audrey Thomason called me the other day and asked if I would be interested in volunteering at Haven House. You know, the women's shelter?"

He nodded. "What did you tell her?"

Laurel shrugged. "I told her I would think about it. She said no one would understand what the women there have gone through like I would, and like she does."

"She's right."

Laurel nodded. "Maybe I could do something like that someday. But most of the time I still feel as if I could be a resident there myself—even now, and it's been months since...and how am I supposed to convince women to leave their abusive husbands and boyfriends? I never left mine. I'm only free now because he died."

"Are there counselors there you could talk to?" Boyd laid the dishtowel aside as she turned the taps off and dried her hands. "Maybe that would be a better place to start rather than just jumping right in as a volunteer." He reached for her hand and stroked his thumb across the knuckles. "It might help to talk to someone."

Laurel sighed and nodded. "Someone like you?"

"You can always talk to me." He raised her hand to his lips and pressed a kiss to the back. "But that's not really what I meant."

"I know." She turned her hand and pressed her palm to his cheek, then raised fingers to touch the wavy, golden brown hair at his temple. He possessed such a kind, gentle nature, and yet he was tall, broad-shouldered, and strong. He was smart and educated — a doctor, no less. And he stood in her small, outdated kitchen helping wash dishes, sincerely interested in what she thought and how she felt. How could this even be possible?

His green eyes searched hers for a long, quiet moment. Were it not for the boys in the next room, he would kiss her. The sweet anticipation of a moment later when he might be able to follow through twisted her insides into giddy little knots.

The shrill ringing of the cordless phone ruined the moment.

But Boyd smiled. "Do you think the boys would let me join them in their game?"

"I think they'd be thrilled if you did."

Laurel picked up the phone as he left the room.

Karen's voice greeted her when she answered.

"Well, I guess y'all aren't coming to see me this afternoon."

Laurel checked her watch. "It's only two o'clock." She glanced into the living room to see Joshua eagerly make room for Boyd and hand over his game controller. "I didn't realize you expected us at a particular time."

"Well, you're usually here before now."

"Yes, but lunch took longer today than usual."

A sudden boisterous cheer went up from all the boys in the other room. The commotion warmed her heart even in the face of the terse silence at the other end of the line.

"Do you have company?"

"Yes. We invited a friend to have dinner with us after church. But we still intend to come over to your house this afternoon."

Another cheer went up. Boyd's laughter was unmistakable.

"Does this friend's name happen to be Boyd Wendall?"

Laurel drew in a deep, silent breath. She would not lie and say no. But the identity of her guest was none of her mother-in-law's business and confessing it would only fan the flames of her anger. It would also make it seem like her friendship with Boyd was a shameful secret. "Yes." She answered finally, knowing that her only option was total honesty without evasion.

Karen already knew where Laurel's friendship with Boyd was probably headed. And she'd made it clear that she did not approve. Nothing new there.

"I see." Karen's clipped answer did not bode well.

"We will be over later, Karen. Within a couple of hours."

"Don't bother. It's clear, now that Tommy's gone, you're eager to replace him. I know you have a lot of work to do there, setting your trap for the next man...now that you've got my son out of the way."

"Karen—" Laurel's intended plea for Tommy's mother to listen to reason was silenced by the click of a disconnected call.

Another raucous cheer came from the living room, followed by overly loud adolescent boy shouts and protests as the game seemingly turned in someone else's favor.

Laurel didn't want Karen to be left out of her grandsons' lives. But how much ugliness was she expected to take for the sake of a woman who had never liked her or approved of her? There was nothing she could do about Karen's refusal to make peace with her. Somehow, she knew there would never be fond affection between them. But the joy in her very own living room—her happy, thriving sons, the doctor who seemed to truly care for her—all of that called to her now, and she followed the call to join them and put aside her trouble with Karen until another day.

~*~

"I can't believe it's nearly dark." Boyd stretched and watched Laurel as she cleared pizza boxes from the coffee table, taking them to the kitchen and then returning. "And you let me stay all day."

She smiled and started sorting the Monopoly money that lay scattered around the game board. "I'm glad you could stay. The boys have never played Monopoly before."

"Well then, Joshua should go into the real estate business when he grows up." He leaned forward and gathered game pieces, adding them to the box. "He's a tycoon in the making."

Laurel laughed softly, and the sound of it struck him again as a new sensation. "I'm surprised they stuck it out to the end. If there's one thing I never could stand about Monopoly, it's how long it takes to play. I would always get bored and make stupid moves just to lose so I wouldn't have to play anymore."

"It does take some time." He watched her long, slender fingers as she put the lid on the box and set it aside.

"Thank you for finishing the game. I think it meant a lot to them."

Each move she made on her way through the room—picking up glasses, restacking the Sunday newspaper—reminded him of a dancer's natural grace. She was quiet and light on her feet, seeming almost as if gravity didn't have the same effect on her that it did on everyone else.

Laurel finished tidying the room, and then turned to look at him. The activity had raised a rosy tint to her cheeks, and a few tendrils had escaped the braid that hung over one shoulder.

Boyd longed to turn the rest loose and watch it fall in the soft, carefree curls he'd glimpsed once before. But he checked the impulse before it grew into something irresistible. "I should go." He stood. "Thank you for lunch."

"Thank you for dinner." She inclined her head toward the plated remnants of the pizza on the coffee table and followed him to the door.

"Well…" He turned to face her, reaching for one of her loose curls and wrapping the silky strands around one finger. "It was my pleasure."

Her eyes narrowed and a hint of a smile curved her mouth.

"You don't believe me?"

"I've just never heard anyone say that so honestly before—as if it really brings them pleasure to do something for someone else."

"It's only pizza. But it does actually bring me a great deal of pleasure to do something for you and your boys."

She observed him for a long moment, her gaze searching his face as if for some specific information. "Is that why you became a doctor? Because you like to do things for people?"

Boyd straightened and shrugged. "Maybe. I don't know. I probably went into medicine more because it was expected of me. My father was—is—a heart surgeon. But I think the field suits me. I do like to help people."

"So how did your father react to the lawsuit?"

"My father has faced a settlement or two of his own during the course of his career. So, he understood. It's not an uncommon thing. For me, it just happened so early on…" He let his voice trail off with another shrug and glanced over her shoulder, his gaze lighting on a framed picture of Laurel, Tommy, and the boys.

Appearances really could be deceiving. If he took the picture at face value—the strong, handsome man and his smiling wife and children—he'd assume they'd been an ordinary, loving family. But he knew the truth. He'd been there that night at the hospital when doctors and nurses buzzed around her, treating the injuries intentionally inflicted by the one who was supposed to love and protect her. He glanced back to find her watching him. "How'd you end up with him?"

Laurel also looked at the picture. "I was young…seventeen when I met him. Well, my life hadn't been ideal, but even so, you know kids. They never think anything really bad can happen to them.

"I'd spent most of my life up to that point in foster homes where I knew I wasn't loved. I might have been liked and treated nicely, I tried hard to please, and I never caused trouble, but..." Her voice trailed off and she shrugged. "I wanted to be loved. And Tommy loved me. So I jumped out of the frying pan and into the fire, as they say. I married him as soon as I turned eighteen. I was about to come to the end of my time in the foster care system, and I was fairly terrified about what might come next for me. It seemed like a better alternative than being alone. And for most of my marriage I felt that way—like I was better off with Tommy, here in this house, than I would have been out there on my own. And I don't guess I ever felt like I really deserved anything better."

"When did that change?"

"About four years ago, when I trusted Christ." She smiled softly. "He's changed me so much. If Tommy had been killed before then, I would have fallen apart. I never would have been able to stand on my own two feet and take care of my boys. I'm afraid to think what might have happened..." She fell silent suddenly and tears pooled in her eyes. "Really, Boyd. They might have ended up with Karen or in foster homes, like me. I wouldn't have been strong enough to keep everything together."

Boyd took her hand and ran his thumb along the soft, warm skin of her knuckles.

"God saved me. He rescued me, and changed me."

He never would have imagined such a thing about her. Boyd had admired Laurel for a while. Admittedly, longer than he should have. He'd only ever seen angelic beauty, quiet dignity, and unearthly strength. And he could see now how all of those qualities had come from her relationship with God. He brushed hair back and pressed a soft kiss to her forehead. "Can I call you tomorrow?"

"I'll be disappointed if you don't."

~*~

"Dr. Wendall, I want your assurance that this procedure will go without a hitch of any kind, and that Elaine will be up and around in short order."

Boyd smiled warmly at Miss Laura. She wasn't being bossy, just concerned for the health and well-being of this niece who had come to be such a big part of her life over the past few years.

"Miss Laura," Boyd took hold of her hand in as reassuring a manner as he could. "You know I can't make any guarantees. But gall bladder surgery is a fairly routine procedure. I know your surgeon, I trust him, and highly recommend him. I wouldn't have referred Elaine to him otherwise."

Miss Laura squeezed his hands. "Thank you, Doctor."

Boyd stepped to Elaine's bedside and laid a hand on her shoulder. "As for being completely back to normal, I'd expect it to take a few weeks. You might be a little sore where the incisions are. But, if the surgery goes without a hitch…" He shot a glance back to Miss Laura. "…as I expect it will, you should be home in your own bed tonight, and feeling pretty good by tomorrow."

Elaine seemed quieter than usual; pensive and worried, so he sat in the chair beside her.

"Truly, Elaine. It's a routine procedure. I don't expect any complications."

"I know." Her expression relaxed and she smiled. "It's not that. It's just…I just wish Justin was here. Last time I was in the hospital I was having the twins, and then after they were born they were here, so I didn't have time to think about..." Her voice trailed off and a haunted expression emerged.

Boyd knew exactly what she was thinking about.

So many of his days blended from one to another in their routine way. But that night...the night she was remembering and the days that followed...would remain forever etched, unfading, in his memory. Elaine had been brutally attacked. And Justin, who had been shot in the chest defending her, had arrived at the ER clinging very loosely to life.

Boyd had never told Elaine just how close they'd come to losing Justin. He'd never told her how certain he had been, even after Justin had been flown to a better equipped hospital and taken to emergency surgery, that he wouldn't survive. He knew miracles happened, and people had been known to beat the odds and pull through under similar circumstances. But he'd never been a witness to such a thing before.

Justin should not have survived that gunshot wound. But he did survive. And he completely recovered.

"Sorry I'm late." The sound of Justin's voice seemed to chase the memories away entirely. "The twins needed a little settling down before I left them at Mom's."

Elaine smiled, fully at ease now. "It's their first sleepover at Grandma's. I don't know who's more excited."

Boyd stood and shook Justin's hand. "Well." Boyd glanced from Elaine to Miss Laura. "I'll be back to check on you in a few hours."

"Will you pray with us before you go, Doctor?"

Miss Laura stretched out a hand to him, and another to Elaine.

"Yes. Of course." Boyd took her hand and bowed his head as Justin prayed for God to guide the surgeon's hands, for a quick and complete recovery, for no complications, for stamina for his mother in watching after their toddlers. Then he thanked God for the blessing of their life together as a family, their home, their health, their lives. Lastly, he thanked God for Boyd and his friendship.

An achy lump formed in Boyd's throat as he listened to Justin's prayer, feeling certain now, for the first time ever, that this place was his home, and his life here had been intended all along. He'd become a part of the fabric of this community, and people here relied on him in more ways than he'd realized before.

Justin's soft amen was echoed by the small group.

Then Boyd excused himself from their company. He stood outside the door, listening for a moment to the soft murmur of voices inside. He wasn't a part of their family, but he wasn't the total outsider he'd always felt like either. He belonged here.

"Hey, Doctor Wendall." A nurse breezed past him on her way down the corridor. "How are you today?"

"I'm well today, Reva. Thanks."

He turned to go the opposite direction, back to the office for a few hours to see a few more patients. After that, he'd come back here to check on Elaine. Then he'd head home where he'd call Laurel and ask when he could see her again.

"Dr. Wendall?" A voice from behind stopped him and he turned.

"Yes." Boyd answered, trying to place the face of the man who'd called him back.

"Dr. Boyd Wendall?"

The man held out an envelope and, without thinking, Boyd reached out to take it.

"That's for you." The man brushed past him and headed for the exit.

Boyd stared down at the seemingly benign package in his hands. But he didn't need to open it to know he'd just been served. And there was no doubt that the envelope contained paper work informing Boyd that he was once again being sued.

11

This visit to Karen was overdue by a few days.

Laurel pulled the strap of her shoulder bag onto her shoulder and stood for a moment staring at the nondescript little house where Tommy had spent his formative years. Sunday had been the last time she'd spoken to her mother-in-law, and that had ended with Karen hanging up on her in an angry huff. Maybe she should have called if only to make sure they'd be welcome. But they'd never needed an invitation before.

T.J. stepped out of the car and softly, deliberately closed the door. He hadn't wanted to come. He was as finished with Karen as he had been with his father on the evening he pointed the shotgun at him in the kitchen.

Laurel understood. But she still hoped that God's redeeming love could touch Karen before it was too late; before her grandsons were grown and didn't have anyone to make them come visit her. Maybe they were meant to be the light that shone into Karen's life and showed her a better way to live.

T.J. headed for the stoop, head down, shoulders slumped, more of a child in that moment than the man he was beginning to resemble.

Laurel smiled and glanced at Joshua, who shrugged and followed his brother inside.

Karen's voice rose in what sounded like a cheerful greeting. Hopefully, she'd forgiven them for having

Boyd come to dinner on Sunday. It sounded as if she had.

"Well, now." Karen exclaimed when Laurel stepped across the threshold. "What a nice surprise. I'll just get something on the stove for us if y'all can stay for supper."

"That would be very nice, Karen. Thank you." Laurel dropped her bag by the front door and followed her mother-in-law to the kitchen.

"You look exhausted, Laurel." Karen pointed her to a chair at the kitchen table. "Could you use a cup of coffee?"

"I sure could." Laurel sat.

The boys headed down the hall. It used to be they'd hide there, back when their father had been alive. They still went straight back after greeting their grandmother, but now it seemed more of a habit than anything else.

"Long day?"

Laurel glanced back at Karen, who started the coffee pot. All she could manage was a nod. "The store was busy today. All day, it was so busy. I didn't even get a real break for lunch, just five minutes to scarf down a sandwich and get back to work. Two people called in sick."

Karen's concerned *tsks* rose along with the soft clatter of pots and pans as she prepared to make supper for them.

Laurel pushed back her chair. "Let me help. What can I do?"

"Nothing. You sit right there and get off your feet." Karen set a mug of coffee on the table. "You work hard to support your boys. And I know it's even harder now that Tommy's gone and you're on your own."

Laurel stared into the blackness of the liquid in her mug. She hated the suspicion that edged its way into her mind. There were only two circumstances under which Karen ever spoke in such an affirming way to her. One was when she wanted something, and the other was after Tommy had left evidence of his evil temper on her face.

Laurel sipped the coffee and remained silent. Waiting.

"I'm sorry about the way I spoke to you Sunday." Karen's apology was spoken softly. But it had been given freely, maybe for the first time ever. "I was missing Tommy, and you and the boys, and feeling lonely. And it just sounded like y'all were having such a good time without me."

Laurel didn't say anything. She didn't know what to say. But when she glanced up from her coffee cup to find Karen observing her expectantly, she accepted the apology with a nod.

Then Karen went back to the dinner preparation.

What did this mean? Was the light Laurel had longed for mere moments ago already showing itself in Karen's life? Something about the woman's demeanor was different this evening. Since Tommy's death, she'd been anxious and angry—more so than usual. But now she seemed at peace. And she was humming serenely as she worked.

Laurel simply listened for long moments to the tune she recognized as being an old standard from decades ago even though she couldn't place the title or remember the lyrics. She sipped her coffee, letting the warm, rich brew relax her.

The humming stopped and Karen's voice rose

softly in a question. "Have you spoken to Dr. Wendall lately?"

Disappointment swelled, bringing a mild ache to her throat and casting its pallor across the kitchen. "No. Not since Sunday."

The last thing she'd said to him was that she'd be disappointed if he didn't call the next day. She'd been half teasing, fully expecting him to call when he said he would. But he hadn't called, and her disappointment had been acute.

"He hasn't called you?"

"No." Karen's mild, disapproving hum floated across the space between them like dust caught in a beam of sunlight. "Maybe he's not quite the hero you imagined, running in here after your husband's death to rescue you."

"I never imagined him to be my rescuer." Laurel kept to herself the idea that, with Tommy gone, she no longer needed rescuing anyway. "I imagine him to be my friend."

"A friend who comes to your house and tries to take the place of your children's father."

Laurel breathed deeply and sipped her coffee. She would not let this turn into another ugly argument. That wasn't why she came.

But maybe there was some small glimmer of truth in what Karen said. Not that Boyd was trying to take Tommy's place in their family. But maybe spending all afternoon and evening with them Sunday changed his heart toward them. Maybe he didn't want a woman who had been married before and already had two children that were closer to adulthood than infancy. Maybe he didn't want to feel as if he was taking someone else's place.

Laurel had expected a sweet, tender kiss before he left her house Sunday evening. But all he'd offered was a cool, almost platonic peck on the forehead. Maybe he'd reconsidered and decided he didn't want her after all.

"Maybe it's for the best." Karen didn't turn away from her dinner preparation. Her tone sounded so very sympathetic, but the compassion felt affected.

"Maybe what's for the best?"

"You don't really know what kind of man he is. Maybe he has some kind of ulterior motive. A doctor that could just sit by and watch a man bleed to death on the pavement...what kind of man is that? What kind of designs does he have on you? You just can't be too careful."

"He didn't just sit by and let Tommy bleed to death, Karen." Laurel turned the mug slowly with her fingertips. "You didn't see him at the hospital that night. He was covered with Tommy's blood. He couldn't have been covered in his blood if he'd just sat by and done nothing."

"Well..." Karen's clipped interruption cut her off. "Let's not talk about it tonight. Let's talk about happier things. You've had a hard day, and I just want to make you and the boys a good supper so you can relax and not have to worry about anything." Karen focused her attention and energy on the meal she was making with an intensity she only possessed when she was angry. Clearly she needed to blame someone for Tommy's death—someone besides Tommy or the man who shot him.

Why she focused that need on the person who tried to do something to save him, Laurel would never know. But Karen was making an effort to change the subject, to not fight. And Laurel knew how difficult that was for her, so she would drop the issue in the interest of peace.

Peace, which was really all she'd ever wanted from her mother-in-law.

~*~

Boyd pinched the bridge of his nose, and then dropped his head into his hands. How many times had he prayed in the last three days that this disaster would just miraculously go away? That was probably the most irrational of ways to pray about it. He should pray for strength or peace, he knew. Because that's what he would need. But the truth was he simply did not want to walk through this again. He didn't think he could.

After being served the summons on Monday, he went back to the office and finished his appointments for the day. Later he went back to the hospital to check on Elaine. He'd gone through every motion with a smile pasted in place and words of comfort at the ready for sick and injured patients. But he'd been so dazed he could barely remember any of the details. Everything about the remainder of the day had been normal, and at the same time so completely not normal.

He had waited until he arrived home to tear into the envelope that the process server had placed in his hands. He read the documents, then reread them several times. Then he contacted his insurance company to explain that he was being sued again for medical negligence.

The complainant was Karen Kerr.

Boyd rose from the dining room table where the papers lay spread out, assuring him that it was really happening. He crossed to the kitchen and opened the refrigerator, then stared into it, unseeing. Finally, he pulled out a carton of orange juice and poured a glass full. Where could he go from here?

Blithe Settlement was a small town with nowhere to hide. What would happen to his practice when word of this got out? Clearly, it hadn't gotten out yet, because all his appointments made it to the office Tuesday and today, along with several walk-ins. But when it did...when people found out...would they assume the worst and find other doctors? Would someone do a little research and dredge up the fact that this wasn't the first malpractice suit he'd faced? Would he need to leave here and start over again somewhere else?

And what would happen when the details of this lawsuit came to light. Karen wasn't only accusing him of simple negligence. She was asserting that his intent had been malicious; that he had withheld aid on purpose because he was engaged in an affair with Laurel and he wanted Tommy out of the way. She was making him out to be an opportunist at best, and at worst a murderer.

He barely tasted the orange juice as he drained the glass. He should eat something. It might help him weather this crisis in a better frame of mind, but his gut was twisted so tightly into knots that every supper plan seemed unappealing.

His gaze fixed on the patio outside where he and Laurel had enjoyed their first evening together. What would this lawsuit mean for her? She wasn't the one being sued, but if the community thought that she had been having an affair with him…

This was sure to be a scandal that would affect them both in the worst of ways.

Now he had to decide if he wanted to settle or take his chances in court.

If he settled, the situation would be put to rest quietly. The details of the allegations might not be spread about town, bringing scrutiny and undeserved blame and embarrassment to Laurel and her boys. But he hadn't done anything wrong. There had been no saving Tommy Kerr. And he'd had no relationship with the man's wife that went beyond the norm. He had done nothing wrong, and a sudden desire for justice swelled and left him longing to see this thing through in court; to be vindicated by a jury that would recognize Karen Kerr's allegations for the lies they were.

"Father, please." Boyd sank into the dining room chair again and buried his face in his hands. He didn't know how to pray. The words wouldn't come. But his whole being ached with the need, so he remained, laying his head down on folded arms, eyes closed, repeating the same plea. "Please, Lord."

~*~

Laurel pressed the doorbell button before she had time to rethink her decision. Rethinking it would probably send her scurrying to her car and running back home. There was a reason Boyd hadn't called. It might be better to leave it alone. It wasn't like she would never see him again. But a nagging, unexplainable concern for him had been steadily edging its way into her heart, and she didn't really believe he hadn't called because he'd changed his mind about her. Nothing seemed more unlike him than that possibility. Fickle, the man was not. All evening she had contended with the growing sense of apprehension that something was wrong.

A light came on inside, and through the beveled glass of the door she saw his form approaching. Then the porch light sparked to life, and the door opened.

Something *was* wrong. Weary concern lined his features for an instant before recognition eased it a little. His normally kind green eyes were red rimmed and dim, as if he hadn't slept in days. His golden brown waves, tousled and disheveled, spoke of trouble.

"Laurel…" He was surprised to see her, but not pleasantly so. Still, he swung the door open and stood aside. "Hi. Come in."

She stepped into the marble tiled foyer. The house was dark except for the one light that had come on when she'd rang the doorbell a moment ago.

Boyd stood beside her, hands in his pockets, shirt collar unbuttoned, and stubble glistening on his jaw. Traces of an extremely difficult day shadowed his expression. And now he looked at her expectantly.

"I was worried about you." She fought the impulse to glance away from the intensity in his green eyes as he seemed to search her for something.

Finally, he nodded. "I'll be OK. Do you want to come in and sit?"

She followed him to the living room where he switched on a few lamps.

He pointed her to a place on the sofa, and she lowered herself into the cool leather, dropping her purse on the floor beside it.

"It's good that you stopped by, actually." He stepped out of the room for a moment. When he came back he laid a few papers out on the coffee table in front of her, then he took a seat beside her.

"When you didn't call Monday..." Laurel stalled and shook her head. She didn't want to accuse him of anything. He didn't have to call her if he didn't want to. "I just started to worry. I do that sometimes."

A hint of a smile softened the lines of his mouth. "I'm sorry. I should have called. I just...when all this came up..." He swept a hand toward the coffee table indicating the papers. "But I do need to talk to you about it, because it will affect you, too—" He stopped abruptly and pressed his lips together into a thin line as he took a deep breath, trying to control some kind of sudden emotion.

Laurel laid a hand on his arm, alarm pulsing through her heart.

"And if you feel like you need to extricate yourself from the situation, I'll understand."

She shook her head. "What situation?"

"All this." He picked up a page and handed it to her.

She took it and let her eyes skim over the very official looking document. Boyd's name was there, and Tommy's, and Karen's. But she couldn't make sense of what it said. She glanced back at his face, embarrassed to admit that she could not interpret the information on the page, especially since he seemed to assume that she knew what he was talking about. "Boyd, I don't know what this means. What is this?"

He edged a little closer and took the page from her hand. "This is a lawsuit. I was served Monday at the hospital."

"A lawsuit? For what? By whom?"

"Karen is suing me for medical negligence in the death of her son. Your husband."

Laurel couldn't stop the shock of tears that sprang forth. She drew her hand away, stung by what sounded like an accusation.

"She's alleging that I didn't meet the standard of care that might have saved his life. Given that I'm a physician, she's charging that I could have done more and didn't because I didn't want him to live."

Laurel raised a hand to her mouth and bit down on her thumbnail.

Karen had said some wild things along those lines in the months since Tommy's death. But surely, that had just been the grief speaking through her. Surely, she didn't really believe those things to be the case.

"Laurel, she's saying we were having an affair."

"But that's not true."

"You mean you didn't know anything about this?"

"No." She gasped, realization dawning. "You don't think I had anything to do with this, do you?"

"No. I know you didn't." He shook his head, softening. "I'm a little surprised you didn't know about it. When you said you were worried about me, I figured Karen had told you."

"The boys and I had supper with her tonight. She didn't say a word about it."

But now Karen's sweet mood and freely bestowed forgiveness made sense. She would be getting the justice she thought she deserved, even though Tommy's death itself seemed like more fitting justice than anything that might result from a spiteful and completely bogus legal action. Karen couldn't possibly win this lawsuit. But dragging Boyd through it anyway was so like her.

Laurel reached for his hand, and his fingers closed around hers as if he'd been treading water for hours and she was the one thing that could keep him from going under. The intensity of his reaction split her heart in two.

"So, when you said you'd understand if I wanted to extricate myself from the situation...did you think I'd walk away? Like your fiancée?"

"I didn't know." Boyd leaned back into the soft leather of the sofa. "This lawsuit will involve you in a way the last one never involved her."

Laurel slipped off her flats and tucked her feet beneath her as she turned to face him.

"If I settle, the lawsuit goes away pretty quietly—if Karen would be content with money. But if she won't, or if I decide not to settle and the whole thing goes to court...you'll be deposed and called to testify. And it won't matter that you're Karen's daughter-in-law. Her lawyer's job will be to make a jury believe that we were having an affair, and that I let Tommy die, and that you might have been complicit."

"But none of that's true."

He shook his head. "It won't matter. There's no way to prove an affair because there wasn't one. But I had feelings for you—feelings that other people knew about—people who would probably be called to testify. And we're seeing each other now. And that might be enough to make a jury see it her way."

Laurel kept quiet the thought that she should probably go now, and that they shouldn't see each other again until the lawsuit was resolved. Boyd was right. They'd both had feelings for each other since before Tommy's death. And now they were seeing each other openly. He had been sitting beside her in church—for everyone to see—for a few Sundays now.

No one had said anything about their budding relationship being inappropriate. There had been smiles of encouragement, and maybe even approval. But did it make them look guilty of doing something wrong?

She moved closer and laid her head on his shoulder, not knowing what to say—how to comfort or counsel him. Only Sunday he had told her that lawsuits against doctors weren't actually unusual. But to her, this was unthinkable. Not only that he was being sued again, but by her mother-in-law, and for no other reason than bitter spite.

Karen knew Tommy as well as anyone. She'd warned and worried that his lifestyle might one day get him shot or sent to prison. And what could she possibly have against the doctor who tried to save his life? The answer was nothing.

He slipped one arm around her shoulders and pulled her closer. Then he raised the other hand to toy with the end of her braid.

"Boyd?"

"Hmm?" She felt the response in the rise and fall of his chest.

"I don't think this lawsuit is about you at all."

He glanced sharply at her, his brows drawing together in confusion.

"Karen knows there was nothing you could do to save Tommy. I think she might be trying to get back at me."

"For what?"

"For not being devastated that Tommy's gone."

Boyd drew in a deep breath and let it out slowly as

if considering.

"She's never approved of me. But she's been especially nasty since Tommy died. I guess when he was alive she kept quiet so she wouldn't upset him. But we've had a few ugly encounters recently."

"What do you mean?"

Laurel lifted one shoulder and glanced away for a moment. "Sometimes it seems as if she's trying to pick up where he left off, at least where the name calling is concerned. And, I don't know, I've just kind of felt like, now that Tommy was gone, I shouldn't have to take any abuse from anyone anymore. I might not have been the perfect wife, but I did the best I could—I really did."

A mix of responses played across his face, making her think he didn't know how to respond to the increasing fervor in her tone. She took a breath and dialed it back.

"She's picked up Tommy's tradition of calling me hateful names. She accuses me of being happy that he's gone…and now that I think about it, she did make a comment about both of us somehow planning what happened to Tommy. I told her that the only plan I'd been making was for the boys and I to leave him—"

"Wait. You told her you were planning on leaving Tommy?"

"Yes. And I shouldn't have said anything. It was unkind. But she was just being so hateful—"

"Is that true? Were you planning on leaving him?"

She nodded. "We had just decided that night—the night Tommy was killed. I was planning to give my notice at work the next day, and we thought we'd rent a trailer and pack a few things and leave."

"So, if Tommy hadn't been killed, you would be

gone now?" Boyd traced her jaw line with a finger.

"More than likely, yes."

A burdened sigh escaped as he relaxed back into the sofa. For a long moment, he stared across the room into the cold, empty fireplace. A muscle along his jaw twitched. She laid her head on his shoulder again and took his hand in hers.

"What do you think I should do?" he asked quietly. "Do you think I should settle, or should I see it through?"

Laurel didn't know how to advise him. She wasn't educated like he was. She didn't know the first thing about lawsuits and lawyers and courts of law. But it seemed to her as if settling out of court implied guilt. And Boyd had done nothing wrong. So it seemed wrong that he should have to live with whatever stigma might come as a result of settling this lawsuit. "I don't think you should settle."

"You don't?"

She shook her head. "If Karen wants to get back at me, she won't settle for money. She doesn't want me to be happy. She doesn't want to see my life improve as a result of Tommy being gone. She wants me to be as miserable as she is. And, for her, that means hurting you because she can see how happy you make me."

He pulled her closer and pressed a kiss to the top of her head.

"She can't lash out at me directly because I have her grandsons, and she wouldn't risk losing them. But if she can plant the seeds of doubt about you in the community...I guess she figures that will hurt us both."

He drew in another deep breath. "All right, then. Tomorrow I'll call a lawyer."

12

Laurel pulled the keys from the ignition and laid a hand on T.J.'s arm before he could open his door and step out of the car. Sinewy muscles tensed beneath her touch, then relaxed as he complied with her unspoken request to calm down.

"We'll talk to her." Laurel's softly spoken plan didn't seem to put him further at ease. "Maybe she will listen to reason. Maybe she's just still so deep in her grief over your father's death that she isn't thinking about what she's doing."

Her son's jaw tensed and twitched, but he didn't say a word.

She had debated whether or not she should tell the boys about last night's conversation with Boyd. Their relationship with their grandmother was already on shaky ground, while their admiration of Boyd increased daily. Telling them what Karen had done would only serve to make them angry with her.

But she'd arrived home from Boyd's house last night to find T.J. waiting up for her.

Evidently, his heart had been burdened for the doctor as well, and he was eager to be assured that all was well.

Laurel hadn't been able to hide her distress. And there had been enough trying to hide the ugliness of life from boys who were clearly old enough to recognize it anyway. So she'd told them the whole story.

T.J.'s fury had seethed ever since.

Joshua had been quiet, but not really angry.

"Let's not go in loaded for bear with our guns blazing, OK?" Laurel gave his arm a gentle squeeze. "I don't think that will help, and it could make things worse."

He relaxed and nodded, grinning slightly at her analogy.

Once inside the house, Joshua when straight back to the boys' usual spot. But T.J. followed Laurel into the kitchen.

Karen sat in her usual place at the kitchen table sipping her late afternoon cup of coffee.

"Well, what a nice surprise." She set her cup down and pushed her chair back. "Can I fix y'all something to eat?"

"No. Thank you."

Karen's gaze shifted from Laurel to T.J., suspicion clouding her features. "Have a seat then."

Laurel pulled out a chair and sat, then motioned for T.J. to do the same.

Karen didn't say a word, but she drew in a deep breath and let it out again dramatically, speaking volumes in a gesture intended to make its recipient feel guilty for being such an abusive, hard-to-live-with person. Karen had always been a master manipulator.

And Laurel had learned to let it roll off with relative ease. But now she nearly snapped. Now she felt contempt, maybe for the first time in her life. "I spoke with Boyd last night."

"Oh?" Karen folded her arms on the table and cast her glance guiltily into her coffee cup, but her tone was pure innocence, as if she didn't know exactly where this conversation was headed.

"Why are you suing him?"

"We don't need to discuss this in front of T.J. It doesn't concern him."

"It *does* concern me—"

Laurel again laid a hand on his arm, and he quieted.

"Boyd has become a good friend to us." Laurel glanced at T.J. who was clearly, deeply offended on Boyd's behalf. "He's more than a friend to us, actually. He's very dear and special. And we just can't understand why you would want to hurt someone who means so much to us. Someone who tried to save Tommy's life after he'd been shot during a drunken fight in a convenience store parking lot."

"So you talked to Boyd, then you went home and told the boys?"

"Did you think you could follow through with a lawsuit like this, and go to court, and have me called to testify, and maybe even have T.J. and Joshua called to testify…did you really think you could go through with all that and have them not find out?"

"He is a doctor. He should have done more. He *could* have done more, he just didn't want to."

"That is simply not true."

"Well, of course you'd say it's not true. He did it for you. It makes sense that you would protect him."

Laurel sighed and glanced at T.J.

Angry red splotches covered his face. He was holding tight to the reins of self-control.

"Do you seriously believe that Boyd and I were having an affair? Seriously? Because, if that's your reasoning, then you've accused me too."

"You said you were thinking of leaving Tommy."

Karen nearly shrieked. "You didn't care what happened to him at all. You had already set your sights on Boyd Wendall. Tommy knew it, and so did I."

"And when would I have had this affair?" Laurel squeezed her eyes shut for a second, hoping that reason would speak sense to her mother-in-law. "I went to work and I came home. I was always either at work, or at home, or with the boys, or with Tommy. When exactly did this torrid affair take place?"

"You know, Laurel, I've never had an affair. I was faithful to my husband. I wouldn't know how to go about carrying one out."

Clearly, reason wouldn't work.

Karen was convinced that her indignation was righteous.

"I came here to ask you to drop the lawsuit. You are hurting people. You're hurting Boyd and me. You're hurting T.J. and Joshua. If you proceed with this, you will tear what remains of this family apart."

"Is that some kind of threat?"

"No, Karen, it's not a threat."

"Because if you think you can threaten me, you're wrong."

T.J. pushed his chair back abruptly and stood. "This isn't right, Grandma. Stop it. Drop the lawsuit."

"Or what?" Karen's glance turned into a glare as she fastened it onto T.J. "Or you'll never speak to me again? You'll leave this house and never come back? Don't you know that will only make me fight this battle harder, and it won't help your precious doctor any."

This confrontation was quickly devolving into something much uglier than Laurel ever intended. T.J. hadn't threatened to quit speaking to his grandmother, although that might end up being a natural consequence of Karen's actions. And Laurel certainly hadn't come here expecting to threaten anything of the kind. What sort of good would that accomplish?

If Laurel denied Karen access to her grandsons, it wouldn't persuade her to drop the lawsuit. It would only make her dig in and fight harder. Boyd would still have to go through it, and that was what Laurel wanted to avoid.

An outpouring of kindness…

The idea drifted through her consciousness, and she knew instantly that it was the one and only thing that would even stand a chance of solving this problem. She also knew that the idea hadn't come from herself. Her feelings toward her mother-in-law were anything but kind at the moment.

But kindness was something Karen had probably never experienced. Certainly not from her husband or children. And not from the folks in this town either. Since Laurel had known her, Karen had been the object of ridicule and contempt for most people she knew; pitied because she'd tied herself to an abusive husband, and despised for raising four of the worst trouble making kids in town.

Kindness might be just the thing to change Karen's heart.

"I will drop the lawsuit."

Laurel snapped back to attention at Karen's quietly uttered statement, then she glanced at T.J. to find him staring at his grandmother in complete shock.

"On one condition."

The ember of hope was extinguished. Of course, there would be a condition. Every good thing from Karen was conditional. The only unconditional things she gave were guilt and manipulation.

"What's the condition?"

"That you never see Boyd Wendall again." Karen looked up from her coffee and leveled a bitter glare on Laurel. "You don't go to his house. He doesn't come to your house. You don't go out together. He doesn't spend any more time trying to take Tommy's place in the boys' lives. You don't sit with him at church and pretend to be the kind of woman he could be satisfied with. And find another doctor to take care of the boys when they're sick."

Laurel couldn't find words to respond. She reached deep inside to find the reins of self-control that T.J. had had a handle on through the whole conversation, but they were elusive. She pushed her chair back, rose slowly, and turned to go.

"Go on ahead and talk to Boyd about it." The quiet rage in Karen's voice stopped Laurel before she could leave the kitchen. "I know you will. But tell him this for me: Tell him that I won't settle out of court for any amount of money. And that if we go to court, everyone in town will get to hear all about his other lawsuit. The one that made him lose his place at his practice in Houston and run here so he could hide away and continue his habit of malpractice on the folks in Blithe Settlement. It will ruin him. And he'll have to leave here, just like he had to leave there."

T.J. stood beside Laurel, and Joshua stepped out of the hallway where he'd been hiding out listening to every word. Now it was her oldest son who laid a calming hand on her shoulder.

"Well..." Laurel's voice trembled and her heart pounded painfully. "If that should happen, I guess there won't be anything left in this town that could

stop me from taking the boys and going with him."
The last thing Laurel saw before she turned and left
Karen's house was her mother-in-law's victorious
smirk fading into an expression that resembled
something a little more like concern.

~*~

Laurel pulled into her driveway, shifted into park,
and killed the engine. How was she supposed to pour
kindness out onto Karen when she was being so
hateful?

"What will you do?" T.J.'s question filled the small
interior of the car, and Laurel turned to him. "Did you
mean it when you said we would go with Dr. Wendall
if he left?"

"I'm sorry, T.J., I shouldn't have said that. I
promise you, that is not a decision I would make
without your input. I was angry. Besides which, if
Boyd did decide to leave town, it might be as much to
get away from me as the lawsuit. Seems like I'm the
whole reason he's going through it."

"What did Grandma mean about his other
lawsuit?" Joshua, who always heard everything, stared
up the street at Boyd's approaching truck.

"Before he came here he was sued for malpractice
by a patient in Houston."

"What does that mean?"

"The patient was sick and died, and his family
sued Boyd."

"Why? Did he do something wrong?"

"I don't know, honey. I don't think so, even
though Boyd does. But sometimes, when a person is
grieving, they feel like they just want to blame

someone. Sometimes there is someone to blame, and sometimes there isn't. And sometimes the wrong person gets blamed."

"But what will happen if everyone in town finds out about that lawsuit? Won't it be bad for his business? Will he have to leave?" Joshua's voice cracked

Laurel met his tearful gaze in the rearview mirror. "Yes. It will hurt him very much. That's why your grandmother wants to use it against him. And, depending on how people react, he may feel like he needs to move away and start over somewhere else— which would be a shame and a big loss for our town because he's a very good doctor."

"But if you don't go out with him anymore, Grandma will drop the suit, and everything will be OK for him."

Laurel nodded and sighed as Boyd parked his truck against the curb.

"But you love him." T.J. watched Boyd's truck as well.

She swallowed back the achy onslaught of tears and nodded again.

"I wish you had never married Dad," Joshua whispered.

"Don't wish such a thing, son." Laurel turned to meet his gaze. "If I hadn't married your dad, then I wouldn't have you guys. And having you guys is worth way more than what I went through with him— or will go through with your grandmother."

Boyd stepped out of his truck and leaned back against the cab, watching them.

Laurel knew better than to think of him as perfect. He was only a man—undeniably handsome, with his gold-brown waves and clear green eyes, square jaw, and cleft chin. His broad shoulders suggested strength and protection and provision. All of that made him perhaps the most handsome man she'd ever seen. But his kind, compassionate heart made him the most beautiful person she'd ever known.

Her own heart sagged with the weight of the choice she had to make now. She could stand beside him through this ordeal and watch him suffer, knowing she could stop it. Or she could tell him she never wanted to see him again and make it all go away.

"So, what will you do?" T.J. asked again.

She drew in a deep breath and mustered a smile. "I'm going inside and cook you all supper. Then I'll enjoy the company of three wonderful men. And I'll try really hard not to think about your grandmother or her lawsuit until much later."

Although she intended to make dinner for all of them, after the confrontation she'd just had with Karen, Laurel was relieved when Boyd revealed a sack filled with fried chicken and potato salad from the grocery store. They sat down to a comforting meal within fifteen minutes.

The shadow of Karen's actions shifted around the kitchen as they ate.

Still, Laurel felt peace and enjoyed watching and listening to Boyd and her boys as they got to know each other. Part of her questioned the wisdom of allowing the relationship among the three to deepen.

T.J. glanced at her once or twice, seeming to feel the same concern.

But Joshua's uncharacteristic exuberance during the meal made it impossible for her to cut it short.

But they could only sit for so long once the meal had been finished.

Laurel needed to clean up the dinner mess, and the boys had homework.

"How was your math class today?" Laurel cleared leftovers and dishes so T.J. could make room for his books.

He shrugged and growing apathy tugged one corner of his mouth back. "OK, I guess. As good as it could go."

"Are you having trouble in math?" Boyd cleared another load of dishes and carried them to the sink.

"I just don't get it. And the teacher isn't any help. He doesn't like to go back and explain things over again. But even if he did, it wouldn't matter because I didn't get it the first time."

Boyd's gaze met Laurel's and she tried to smile to keep the mounting helplessness tamped down.

T.J. had always been a good student. But he was struggling in math this year. And he was beyond her ability to help.

"Can I help?" Boyd asked. "I was pretty good at math. Sometimes you just need to have it explained a different way. It's like a puzzle, and you just need to figure out how to solve it."

T.J. grinned and nodded. "It would be a big help if you could."

Boyd took a seat next to T.J. as he opened his backpack and extracted textbooks, notebooks, pencils and paper.

Laurel turned back to the dishes, listening to the low timbre of Boyd's gentle voice explaining mathematical concepts she'd long ago forgotten, if she'd ever known them at all.

Within minutes, T.J.'s voice rose in the sound of complete revelation as a concept clicked and he got it. Question after question followed as T.J. flipped pages in his book.

Boyd answered them all as if he were a math teacher rather than a doctor.

Laurel smiled.

This—a kindhearted man sitting at the kitchen table helping the kids with homework—was like a snippet from the best, most impossible dream she'd ever had.

In the next instant, she thought of Karen and the position she'd had put them in. Animosity the intensity of which she'd never experienced took hold of her soul and began to squeeze the life out. Any future she might have with Boyd was being destroyed deliberately. Not because Karen truly believed that Boyd had done anything wrong, but because she didn't want Laurel to be happy.

~*~

"Thank you for helping T.J. with his math." Laurel set a steaming mug of coffee on the end table and sat beside him on the sofa.

"It was no trouble."

"Maybe not for you." Laurel pulled her feet up and tucked them beneath her. "But it meant a lot to him. This is the first year he's struggled so hard with math. And I think there's a personality conflict of some kind with his math teacher. He likes all his other teachers fine, but this one…"

Boyd nodded. "It'll be good practice for managing in a world where he's bound to find people he doesn't get along with. Sometimes it happens."

Laurel knew that Boyd was speaking in general terms. But she couldn't help thinking of Karen, and how difficult she had always been to get along with. It was easy to blame Tommy's father for the way his children had turned out. His abuse was clearly evident. But Karen, with her extremely manipulative nature, had to share some of the blame.

Boyd's brows had drawn together, and she knew he was thinking about Karen also.

"I went to see Karen today," she said.

His green gaze met hers and he held out a hand to her. "What happened?"

"She told me she won't settle for any amount of money." She laid her hand in his upturned palm and his fingers closed around it. "It's as I thought. This is about her not wanting me to move on and be happy."

"It doesn't matter." Boyd shrugged and stroked the back of her hand with his thumb. "We decided I wouldn't settle anyway, right?"

"Yes. I just thought if I could talk to her, tell her how many people besides me she's hurting by doing this..." Laurel let her voice trail off with a shrug. "I don't know. I'd hoped she might be persuaded to drop it altogether."

"And she couldn't be."

"Actually, she said she would drop it, on one condition."

Boyd's head snapped up and a look of hopeful surprise lit his face. "What condition?"

"That I stop seeing you."

Immediately the hope died and he expelled a long breath. He sat silently for a long moment, staring at their joined hands. "Well, that won't happen, will it?"

An ache rose to her throat. She'd been asking herself the same question since leaving Karen's house. Laurel could end this whole lawsuit for Boyd. All she had to do was send him away and refuse to see him again. She had debated not saying anything about her conversation with Karen, and simply sending him on his way tonight, then refusing to take his calls.

The lawsuit would be dropped, and Boyd could move on with his life with no damage done. But Karen would end up getting exactly what she'd wanted in the first place. Karen would still win. And Boyd, her boys, and, yes, even herself would be left heartbroken in the wake of her mother-in-law's manipulation.

"Will it?" Boyd's hand tightened around hers.

Laurel cast her gaze to the sofa's upholstery and shrugged. "It can end—the whole lawsuit. She'll drop it and it will all be over. You won't have to go through it again. We haven't been seeing each other for very long...I want you to know you have the option."

Boyd withdrew his hand from hers and stood, muscles in his jaw working suddenly as his expression turned grim.

Laurel's heart stopped. She'd made him angry. What an idiot she'd been to speak so frankly. She'd only wanted to give him the freedom to end their relationship. He deserved to know the truth of what Karen had told her today. That this lawsuit wasn't about him at all, and he did not have to put himself through it.

Boyd paced halfway across the room then turned to face her.

Laurel held her breath, knowing with absolute certainty that Boyd was not the kind of man who would jerk her up by the arm and push her around, or strike her across the face with a closed fist. He would not slip a hand around her throat and squeeze just hard and long enough to let her know that he could kill her if he wanted to. Still, something inside of her braced for it. She stood slowly and backed toward the kitchen, her well trained flight instinct engaging before she could switch it off.

He stepped toward her, and blind panic rose from some dark place causing her to counter by taking two very quick steps back. She felt for the wall behind her, preparing to run.

"Laurel?"

She blinked as the sound of his voice seemed to break the curse. The man who stood in her living room was Boyd, not Tommy.

Boyd.

He held out a hand to her and she reached for it, tears stinging. Then she stepped into his open arms and laid her head against his shoulder.

This was not Tommy. He looked different. He smelled different. His arms around her felt completely different.

"Is that what you want?" His deep, gentle voice sounded different. "Do you want me to walk away from you...from us?"

She shook her head.

"Laurel, I'd rather go through it with you than not go through it without you."

She nodded and slipped her arms around his waist, relaxing as his arms closed fully around her. Not until this moment, as she felt the tension drain away, did she realize the weight of the burden she'd carried since leaving Karen's house. Boyd had taken it from her and was willing to carry it himself despite the fact that it had nothing really to do with him.

"Did you call a lawyer?" she asked.

"No." One of his hands made small, comforting circles on her back.

"Why not?"

"I think the Lord told me not to."

She raised her head from his shoulder and looked at him, assessing his expression to see if he was serious.

He was.

"A scripture reference popped into my head this morning. I mean, just from out of nowhere. Exodus 14:14. I had no idea what that verse said. I didn't know if I'd even read that verse before, and it wouldn't leave me. So, I looked it up."

"What did it say?"

"'The Lord will fight for you; you need only to be still.'"

~*~

The Lord will fight for you; you need only to be still.
What did that mean?

The Word had stopped Boyd from making any plans to respond to Karen's lawsuit, but he spent the rest of the week wondering. Did it mean he literally was to do nothing, and simply let events unfold however they would? Or maybe he was supposed to think carefully before he acted, but act nonetheless.

Boyd glanced at the Bible on his knee and opened to the book of Exodus, chapter fourteen. It said the Lord would do the fighting. He should be still. Wait.

Laurel's cool hand covered his, bringing him fully back to the present. The pastor was wrapping up the sermon, and although he had tried to concentrate, Boyd hadn't heard much of it. He glanced at Laurel, then at Joshua and T.J. on her other side.

Whatever happened would impact them as well. But he trusted that God was able to orchestrate an outcome that would be in the best interest of them all. He just couldn't imagine what that could possibly be.

But he would be still.

The service ended and the pleasantly dispersing congregation diverted his thoughts, as did his empty stomach.

"I have a pot roast in the slow cooker if you'd like to join us for lunch." Laurel linked her arm through his. She must have heard his stomach growl.

He found a smile for her and nodded. "I'd like that."

"Excuse me…"

A spoken request for his attention accompanied by a hand on his shoulder made Boyd turn around.

He recognized the man addressing him as a regular church attendee, but Boyd had only seen him here. And he'd only ever spoken to him in the form of a hand shake and a *good morning* during the Sunday morning greeting time. The man—his name was Colin Price—extended his hand and Boyd reflexively reached out to shake it as his mind searched for more details about Colin's identity.

Boyd's heart felt like it slammed against his chest wall as he recalled that Colin Price was a lawyer. Instantly, a wall of suspicion went up, and Boyd withdrew from the handshake. Colin was a regular attendee here; regular enough to be a familiar face. But for how long exactly had he been attending? Boyd couldn't remember.

"May I have a word with you?" Colin asked.

"Yes." Boyd responded cautiously, turning to Laurel. "Y'all go ahead. I'll be over in a few minutes when I'm finished here."

Laurel nodded, concern creasing her brow, and then she turned and led the boys to the parking lot.

"I don't know if you remember me, but my name's Colin Price. I'm an attorney."

Boyd nodded. "I remember."

"I've heard a little about your legal situation, and I just wanted to let you know that I'd be pleased to represent you pro bono if you haven't already secured other counsel."

Boyd took a step back. "You'd represent me for free? Why?"

Colin drew in a deep breath and glanced over Boyd's shoulder for a long moment as if choosing his words carefully. "I want to. I feel as if I'm supposed to."

The sanctuary had emptied and the lights began to go out.

Colin turned for the exit, motioning for Boyd to join him. "This lawsuit feels wrong to me," Colin said. "I've represented doctors in malpractice cases before, so I'd like to volunteer." He paused for a long moment, but clearly had something more to say. "I feel as if God wanted me to offer to represent you. Does that make sense?" Colin reached into his shirt pocket and pulled out a business card.

Boyd took it, swallowing down the rising ache and glancing away to watch the still retreating cars of congregants. "No. It doesn't make sense. But I understand. Thank you."

"My office number is there, and I've written my

cell on the back."

Boyd extended his hand to Colin for another handshake.

"Give me a call." Colin gave him a parting wave, and then headed across the parking lot to the only remaining car aside from Boyd's.

The Lord will fight for you; you need only to be still.

13

Laurel paced to the plate glass window at the front of the lobby and let her gaze survey the bustling morning traffic on the street. The deepening purple leaves of the decorative pear trees across the street, and the brisk wind that tugged a few loose and whisked them away reminded her that fall had fully arrived after a summer that had crawled by.

She refused to yield to the urge to wring her hands, but doing so meant keeping her arms folded tightly and her hands balled into fists.

Boyd continued to try to persuade her to sit, but she couldn't. For weeks she'd been coiled tighter than a spring, and this weekend had been the worst. She'd spent two days on the verge of tears despite the fact that Colin had painstakingly prepared her for today's deposition.

Laurel had prayed for hours, terrified she would say something to make Karen's case stronger, and she'd managed to arrive at a tentative sort of peace. This morning she woke feeling calm and ready. With steady nerves, she made it here to the office.

Then Karen had arrived, drifting through the building's lobby, a wadded up tissue pressed to her nose, face contorted with emotion, and her lawyer's hand comfortingly at her back.

In that moment, Laurel's confidence began to flag, and it weakened further with every second that passed. *Where are You Lord? Where is Your peace?*

"Are you ready?" Colin's soft touch of her elbow nearly caused her to come unwound.

No, she wasn't ready. But she managed to hold herself together. She glanced at Boyd who gave her an encouraging wink. He would go in with her, but he wouldn't be allowed to speak. She'd have to face her mother-in-law alone.

Well, she'd done it before. Just not with lawyers present.

Laurel took a deep breath, nodded and followed Colin to a conference room at the center of which stood a highly polished table. Colin directed her to a seat across from Karen and her attorney, then took a seat beside her.

The court reporter he'd told her to expect sat neutrally at one end.

Laurel glanced over her shoulder at Boyd who settled into a chair against the wall.

"Good morning, Mrs. Kerr." Karen's lawyer addressed Laurel in a warm and friendly manner, putting her instantly at ease.

"Good morning," she replied.

"How was your weekend?"

Laurel blinked and her breath caught. This wasn't simply small talk. The deposition had begun. And Colin had warned her that this was probably exactly how it would begin. The opposing counsel would set a cordial tone, acting as if he liked her and was personally interested in her life, as if he wanted to put her at ease and be her friend.

"It was fine," Laurel voiced her reply cautiously.

Colin had told her not to volunteer any information under any circumstances. Stick to *yes* and *no* answers as much as possible. What else had he said? Suddenly her mind was blank, so she clung to the one piece of advice she could remember.

The warm, seemingly nice attorney sitting across from her was not her friend. His job was to destroy Boyd's reputation and possibly hers as well—not that her reputation had ever been highly prized. She'd never been more to the people of Blithe Settlement than an object of pity and an example of how not to pick a husband. But she would not do anything to make winning this lawsuit harder for Boyd if she could help it.

"You were married to Tommy Kerr for fifteen years. Is that right?"

"Yes."

"And would you say he was a decent husband?"

"No."

Karen's attorney paused for a moment as Karen sniffed and dabbed her eyes with her tissue.

"Why would you say he wasn't a good husband? Didn't he earn a steady paycheck that helped cover the bills?"

"Yes."

"Wasn't he home most every night?"

"Yes."

"What did he do wrong?"

Laurel glanced from her interrogator to Karen, who wouldn't meet her gaze. Was it possible Karen's lawyer didn't know what kind of man Tommy had been, or was this only a part of his strategy? She cast a glance at Colin who gave her an encouraging nod.

"He regularly beat me and sometimes our children."

The lawyer's brow furrowed in concern. "That

must have been a terrible ordeal for you."

Laurel remained silent. That wasn't a question.

"But…aside from that…"

Laurel felt her brows rise and her cheeks flamed suddenly. Did he mean to imply that regular physical abuse did not make Tommy quite bad enough?

An angry witness makes a bad witness. More of Colin's advice drifted through her consciousness, and at just the right moment. Laurel tamped down her indignation and relaxed.

"In what other ways was he a bad husband?"

"He drank too much—"

"Would you say he was an alcoholic?"

"Yes."

"What else?"

"He was regularly unfaithful to me."

"So, in your opinion, would that justify you being unfaithful to him?"

"No."

"So you were never unfaithful to him?"

"No."

There was a long pause during which Karen gave a disgusted little snort.

"Did he ever kill anyone?"

"I don't know."

"Did he ever rape anyone?"

"Other than me, you mean?"

Karen slapped a hand on the table and her face contorted with rage. "That's the most ridiculous thing I've ever heard!"

Her lawyer laid a hand on her arm, and she calmed.

"Other than you," he clarified quietly.

"I don't know."

Silence filled the room as if her admission had come as a shocking surprise and now everyone needed to rethink their strategy. As if Tommy raping her had never been a thought that ever crossed their minds. As if, no matter how badly he treated her otherwise, no matter that he left her bruised and bloody with broken bones, forcing her to have sex with him would be where he'd draw the line.

"Is it true that your son, T.J., once threatened to shoot Tommy?"

Laurel looked at Karen who turned away.

She had never mentioned that day to anyone. And she was certain neither one of her boys would have either. It had to have been Tommy that told Karen.

"Yes. Tommy was attacking me. T.J. was trying to protect me."

"Why was Tommy attacking you?"

It was as if the man wasn't even listening to her answers. It felt as if he was trying to drive the line of questioning to a particular outcome.

Laurel felt anger rise again. "That's just the sort of thing he did. He never needed a reason."

"But that day he had a reason, didn't he?" His cordial, sympathetic demeanor cooled.

Laurel thought back to that day. What had been the reason for Tommy's attack? It took a few minutes, but the details reemerged. "I took T.J. to the doctor. He came home from school sick, and I took him to the doctor."

"Which doctor?"

"Dr. Wendall."

"So, he attacked you for taking your sick son to the doctor? His son?"

"Yes."

"Isn't it true that he attacked you because he suspected you of having an affair with Dr. Wendall?"

"Oh, well, when you put it that way, I guess he was completely justified in throwing me across the room and putting his hands around my throat to choke me."

Colin touched her arm gently. *An angry witness makes a bad witness.*

"Isn't it true you were having an affair with Dr. Wendall?"

"No."

"It's not true?"

"It is not."

The lawyer pressed his mouth into a thin tight line and glanced at Karen, seeming displeased. "But you were aware that Tommy thought you were having an affair with him."

"I was aware that the excuse he used to push and slap and shove and choke me was that he thought I was having an affair. I don't know what he really believed."

"And still you took your other son to the doctor's office the next day, didn't you?"

"Yes. He was sick."

"Even though Tommy asked you not to take him. You took him anyway. Is that right?"

"Joshua was sick. His temperature was a hundred and four. And Tommy didn't *ask* me not take him, he ordered me not to."

"Why not take your son to a different doctor?"

The question stiffened Laurel's spine and made her heart pound. Why hadn't she taken Joshua to another doctor? She hadn't even thought about it at the time. She remembered suggesting to Tommy that he take Joshua to see Boyd, but in her mind, there hadn't been any other option. Boyd was the only man she really trusted, even then.

"Because Dr. Wendall is the boys' doctor."

"Where were you on the night Tommy was killed?"

"At home."

"Were you alone?"

"No."

"Who was with you?"

"My boys."

"What were you doing at home that night?"

Laurel shook her head and tried to remember. "We were just at home. I don't remember exactly what we did. We had dinner. The boys did their homework."

"Isn't it true that you and Joshua and T.J. were making a plan to leave your husband on that night?"

Laurel looked again at Karen.

Karen looked away, and with a sinking heart, Laurel remembered an angry conversation they'd had not long after Tommy died. Laurel glanced at Colin who nodded gently.

"Yes."

"And how did Boyd Wendall figure into your plan to leave your husband?"

"He didn't."

"So, you were planning on taking Tommy's sons and leaving town?"

"My sons, and yes."

"Where were you planning on going?"

"We hadn't decided."

"We, meaning you and Dr. Wendall?"

"We, meaning me and my sons."

"Joshua and T.J. were on board with leaving their father?"

It had been their idea. *Don't volunteer any information...*

"Yes."

Karen's attorney drew in a deep breath and paused for a long moment, shuffling through the papers in front of him until he found one that seemed to hold him transfixed for a moment.

Laurel glanced at Colin who gave her an encouraging smile and laid a hand on her arm.

"I've spoken with a witness that stated you had a very strong reaction to seeing Dr. Wendall at the hospital that night. The night your husband died."

Laurel sat and waited for the coming question, trying with everything in her to remain as unresponsive as possible now.

"The same witness stated that you had a remarkably less strong reaction to the sight of your husband's dead body."

Don't volunteer any information. Make him ask a question, and then answer as briefly as possible. Colin's advice came back in a rush.

"What accounts for the difference in your reactions?"

Laurel closed her eyes, trying to remember the details of that night. The image of Boyd, covered in Tommy's blood returned in graphic detail. So did the fear that had gripped her heart when she'd seen him. "I'd been told that Tommy had been shot. I didn't expect to see Dr. Wendall there splattered all over with blood. I was afraid Tommy had attacked him."

"And what would make you think Tommy would do such a thing?"

Laurel's throat constricted and she cleared it. "He had threatened to kill me a couple of weeks before that...he accused me of having an affair with Dr. Wendall. So, it wouldn't have been outside of his character to do such a thing."

"Do you think it would have been outside of the character of Dr. Wendall to sit by and let Tommy die on the night he was shot?"

"Yes."

"What makes you think so?"

"Dr. Wendall is a good man. He wouldn't do something like that."

"How do you know?"

Laurel shook her head and shrugged. "I just know. I know him."

"How could you know him that well? If he was just your children's doctor, how could you really know what kind of man he was?"

Laurel glanced at Colin, feeling as if she'd stepped into a snare and it was beginning to tighten. How was she to answer that? Karen's attorney was right. There was no way she could have absolutely known what sort of man Boyd was at that point. Except that, somehow, she did.

"You married a man who regularly abused you and your children. You claim that not only was he regularly unfaithful to you but he raped you. If that's true, are you really such a good judge of character?"

No, she wasn't. The snare tightened a bit more.

"Are you aware that Dr. Wendall has been sued for malpractice before?"

Laurel swallowed the ache forming in her throat. "Yes."

"So, you're aware that he has a history of medical

neglect?"

"Um…" She looked to Colin for encouragement, but his furrowed brow only worried her. "I really don't know what that means."

"It means a patient of his in his Houston practice died because of him. Just like your husband died because of him. Are you aware that, before Tommy died, Dr. Wendall had feelings for you that went beyond the norm for a doctor patient relationship?"

Laurel nodded. "Yes." The answer came out as a whisper.

"Given his romantic interest in you and his knowledge of how badly your husband treated you, is it really such a stretch to believe that, despite the fact that Dr. Wendall is trained to save lives, he would take advantage of the opportunity to simply let Tommy die?"

Tears burned and she blinked them back, not knowing how to answer that question. Yes, it had been a stretch to believe such a thing about Boyd. But Karen's lawyer made it sound completely plausible. And how could she know for certain that it wasn't the truth?

"Does Dr. Wendall have some kind of God complex that makes him think he should decide who lives and dies depending on whose wife he wants? Or is he simply an incompetent doctor?

"Objection." Colin interjected, directing his attention to the court reporter. "Calls for speculation. Don't try to answer that, Laurel."

Karen fixed a stony expression on her, and Laurel felt a humiliating tear trail down the side of her cheek. If this was a preview of what the trial would be like, there was no way Boyd could win.

He had done nothing wrong, but Karen's attorney twisted everything that happened, everything was said in such a way that he seemed guilty. Motives had been ascribed to him that couldn't be true, but then again, they could be.

Karen's lawyer wrapped up his questions, but his damage had been done to perfection. He had shaken her confidence in the outcome. Justice didn't always prevail, and she could see how easily this case might be lost.

Karen and her lawyer gathered their things and left Laurel and Colin at the table.

Colin handed her a handkerchief, and Laurel dabbed the tears from her eyes.

"I'm sorry," she whispered.

He shook his head. "You did very well."

Maybe he was being kind. Maybe he didn't want to distress her further. But she was certain she had not done well. This meeting had been worse than any beating Tommy had ever given her. It had felt as if she were the one on trial. And, as far as Karen was concerned, she was.

"Can I go home now?"

Colin nodded and stood, gathering folders, legal pads and his laptop, and then tucking them into his briefcase.

Laurel rose and turned to face Boyd.

His ashen face proved that this interview had been as upsetting for him as it had been for her. And the pained, sympathetic expression made it clear that the information she'd divulged about her relationship with Tommy was what bothered him most. He stood as she approached his chair, and reached for her hand. She could see that he wanted to pull her into an embrace, to comfort her, but she couldn't.

Memories of Tommy had been shaken loose from corners of her mind where she'd tucked them away, and now they swirled mercilessly around her. She simply did not want to be touched right now, by anyone. She wanted to crawl into her bed, burrow under the covers, and weep.

~*~

Boyd wasn't sorry that Tommy Kerr was dead. He had never been sorry about that. But it was becoming more and more difficult to keep from being glad the man was dead; from feeling as if there was profound justice in the way his life had ended.

Boyd raised a hand and knocked softly on Laurel's front door.

He hadn't been able to leave with her after her deposition. Colin needed to go over some details with him, one of which was the fact that Karen was now insisting that T.J. and Joshua be deposed as well. Boyd couldn't fathom what might have happened to make a woman so bitter and hateful that she would be willing to put her family—her grandchildren—through such an ordeal. Maybe she was truly unaware of what kind of son she'd raised. But how could that be?

The door opened and Joshua greeted him with a subdued smile.

"Hi, Dr. Wendall. Come on in."

Boyd stepped inside. "Is your mom home?"

"Yes sir, I'll get her." Joshua closed the door, then slipped past him and headed down the hall.

"Hello, T.J."

Joshua's brother sat on the sofa studying a

textbook.

"Hey, Dr. Wendall."

"How's your mom?" Boyd sat in a chair adjacent.

T.J. closed his book and set it on the coffee table. "She's been in bed since we got home from school."

"Did you guys get something to eat?"

"We had leftovers."

Boyd nodded. "Good."

Joshua slipped back into the living room and sat next to T.J.

"She'll be out in a few minutes."

Both boys sat silently, staring at their knees. The strain of these past few months was clear to see.

"I'm sorry about all this." Boyd said quietly. "If your grandmother would have settled out of court, I would have, so you guys and your mom didn't have to go through it."

"You shouldn't have to settle." T.J. met his gaze. "You didn't do anything wrong. I shouldn't have had them call you that night at the hospital. I wasn't really thinking about how it would look. I just thought that you were a doctor, and I knew you would help. But it just made everything worse."

"Why didn't you call your grandmother?"

"She wouldn't have come. She would have found some excuse not to."

"What happened today, Dr. Wendall?" Joshua's expression pleaded with him to make this whole ordeal stop somehow. "Since Dad died, mom's been different. She's been happy and not scared all the time. But now...it's like he's back again. It's like while we were at school he came back and beat her up again."

Boyd nodded and cleared the scratchy ache from his throat. "That's what today was like for her, I think.

Kind of like he came back and beat her up again."

He heard the closing of the bathroom door in the hall, then the running of water.

"Do you guys visit with your grandmother much?"

T.J. shook his head. "Mom won't see her anymore. She tells us that if we want to see her we can. She'll drop us off and pick us up, but…" His voice trailed off and he shrugged. "I don't want to see her. She doesn't really care about us."

"That's not true, T.J." Laurel said as she joined them. "She does care, she just…" Laurel stood, shaking her head as if she didn't even believe what she'd been about to say. She looked more comfortable now, in her jeans and pullover sweater, than she had earlier. Her dark, loose curls tumbled about her shoulders, recently brushed, but her puffy, red-rimmed eyes betrayed the fact that she'd probably spent a great deal of time this afternoon crying.

"Boys, could Boyd and I speak in private for a few minutes?"

Joshua and T.J. rose and headed down the hall toward their bedrooms as Boyd stood.

"I'm sorry, Laurel." He took a step toward her, hoping she wouldn't shrink away from him as she had earlier.

She reached for his hand. "It's not your fault. None of it. I've managed to drag you down into our mess. I'm the one who should be sorry."

"Karen's attorney wants to depose T.J. and Joshua."

Her eyes widened. "What? Can they do that? What do they think the boys could possibly tell them other than how terrible their father was, and how unsurprising it is that his life ended the way it did?"

"Colin said he'll try to stop it."

She nodded and crossed to the couch and sat.

Boyd followed.

"I wish you hadn't been there that night. I mean, what are the odds that you would be there at the same moment...it's as if God wanted you there on purpose, and why? So that we would have to go through this? So that I would have to relive every vile thing Tommy ever did to me? What is the purpose in that?"

He sat beside her and drew her gently into the circle of his arms. "I don't know what the purpose is." He whispered against her hair and pressed a kiss to her temple. "But I'm sure there is one."

"Do you really think being with me is worth going through it, Boyd? If you go through this trial and you lose, if your patients stop coming to you, if you have to leave here and start over again somewhere else—"

"I love you, Laurel." He pressed his forehead to hers. "If I lose everything, and have to leave here and start all over...as long as you and T.J. and Joshua will go with me then, yes, it will be worth it."

14

If there was anything that Boyd did not want to spend the time or energy to deal with, it was this. He forced a smile and waved at the blonde in the corner booth, and she beamed when she recognized him.

Her phone call last spring informing him she'd be in town had completely slipped his mind in the midst of everything else. But when Annette had called him this afternoon saying she'd be in town in time to meet him for dinner, he vaguely recollected telling her that if she happened to be in town he'd be happy to catch up with her. But that was before this lawsuit came up, making Boyd's daily life a trial to get through.

Now he simply wanted to go home, share a meal with Laurel and the boys, relax, and not think about the deposition scheduled for next week. But Annette was here, wanting to catch up. And if she'd been in touch with his parents at all, they'd have told her about the lawsuit, and she'd want to hear every detail.

Annette stood as he approached, and he couldn't help it when his forced smile morphed into something more heartfelt. She was as beautiful as ever, every hair untouchably in place, skin smoothed to flawless perfection by an expensive line of department store makeup. She wore tight jeans tucked into tall boots and a loose, light blue blouse topped off with a long black sweater. She was, as always, the picture of style and wealth.

"Boyd!" She sounded breathless.

"Hi, Annette."

She wrapped her arms around his neck and he embraced her reflexively. The sugary scent of her perfume transported him back to a time several years ago when his life had held promise and she had been the woman he was certain he'd spend his life with.

"You look good." She stepped back and seemed to take in the sight of him, resting a cool palm against his cheek. "It's unfair how men get better looking as they get older." She paused and her smile faded, brow creasing in concern. "You look tired."

He raised a hand to rub the back of his neck. "I've had a lot going on this year."

"I know. I heard." She slipped into the booth. "Your mom told me you're going through another lawsuit."

He nodded and glanced at the door. Laurel should be here soon. He'd invited her to come along as soon as Annette had called him this afternoon. It wasn't so much that he wanted the two to meet, but he didn't want this meeting to seem like a secret he was keeping from her. And no matter what he did lately, he couldn't shake the nagging feeling that he'd be better off with a witness present.

"So…" Annette glanced around the dining room. "The Prickly Pear is the place to meet around here, is it?"

Boyd's grin spread slowly. "It's a small town."

"I noticed." Her smile was still dazzling. "Honestly, Boyd, I don't know how you've managed to live here for seven years. What do you do when you're not working?"

"I go home, go to church, see friends. The truth is,

establishing my practice took a few years of long hours, so I didn't have a whole lot of extra time. But I've adjusted. I kind of like the slower pace of life here."

The waitress approached and took their drink orders.

Annette ordered a diet soda and Boyd ordered two iced teas, one for himself and one for Laurel.

"Are you extra thirsty, or are you expecting someone else?"

"I invited a friend to join us."

"Oh." Surprise lit her features for a second, along with a measure of displeasure. But she recovered quickly. "So, what about this lawsuit? What happened?"

Boyd shrugged, reluctant to divulge much information. "You come from a doctor's family, you know how it is. Sometimes when people die, those left behind need someone to blame. It helps them process through it, I guess."

"Your mother said the person who died wasn't your patient."

"No. I happened to be at the scene when he was shot. But there was nothing I could have done to save him."

"So his family is blaming you rather than the person who shot him? What about the paramedics, what do they have to say about it?"

Boyd glanced at the door again and shook his head. "It looks as if it's going to trial, so I really can't talk too much about it. Besides, I'd rather not. Tell me what's going on with you. What brings you through Blithe Settlement?"

She dazzled him with another smile.

And for a second he forgot everything else.

"I'm meeting some friends for a ski vacation in New Mexico. Do you remember Carrie Dunbar?"

Boyd nodded and smiled at the mention of their old friend's name.

"Well, she's married now and living in Phoenix. She and her husband are meeting me in Ruidoso for the week."

"So Carrie was willing to leave Houston after all." Boyd traced the wood grain of the table with the tip of a finger, hating the bitterness that swelled so suddenly. "I thought she was as entrenched there as you."

Annette glanced down as the waitress arrived with their drinks and to take their order, giving her a moment to process his barb.

"I'm sorry, Annette." He didn't know where it had come from, and it really wasn't like him to be unkind. But the wound still ached a little.

"Don't be." She shook her head. "What happened to us was my fault. Would it surprise you to know that I never intended our breakup to be permanent?"

"Um, yes." Boyd rubbed a hand across the back of his neck. "Considering you returned the engagement ring, it would surprise me very much."

A regretful sigh slipped from between her pink glossed lips. "I thought you'd come out here for a year, or maybe two, take some time to heal, then come home. I never thought we wouldn't end up together."

"If that's what you thought, why couldn't you have come with me?"

"My job and my family were in Houston. What would I have done here while you were spending long hours building your new practice?"

"Made our home and raised our children,

maybe?"

Her big blue eyes misted and she glanced away.

"I guess I never thought you'd choose a job and a place over me." Boyd took a moment to check his rising frustration. He truly wasn't angry with her any more. But lately he was finding himself a touch more prone to frustration than normal. "I didn't make the decision to move out here capriciously. My life fell apart. I needed a place to start over."

"Then maybe you could start over again, now, back in Houston." Her voice was barely more than a whisper. "Leave this new lawsuit behind. Settle it quietly and come home."

"I'm sorry..." Boyd squeezed his eyes shut for a second and shook his head. "Come...home? It's been seven years. I don't have any connections in Houston, aside from my parents. I couldn't possibly start over there." Or could he?

No telling what might happen at Monday's deposition. And the trial wouldn't begin for weeks. Maybe it wasn't too late to bring the whole thing to an easy end? All Karen Kerr seemed to want was for him to be gone. And here was Annette, beautiful as ever, suggesting how easy it might be to slip right back into that other life—the one he had mourned the loss of for the better part of his time here.

She raised her gaze to his. "Seven years is a long time to be gone. You could find another practice...or start one of your own."

He shook his head and wrapped his fingers around the cool tea glass, dredging his memory for all the reasons he had thought Blithe Settlement might be a good move. "I could have found another practice to join then. That isn't why I moved out here."

"Boyd, I've been seeing someone else." She made the admission as if she expected it to be a great blow.

"So have I."

"He'll be asking me to marry him soon."

Boyd nearly congratulated her before he realized that she really had been keeping him on the back burner all this time. She had expected him to return to Houston and pick up where they'd left off. Now she needed to know where she stood with him in reality, not just in her memory and imagination.

"It's just that if you're going to come home, then maybe..." She raised her sky blue eyes to his. "But if you're not, then I'd like to tell him yes."

Boyd took a breath and found what he hoped was a warm smile for her. If this was really what her visit was all about, then he would make it easy for her. Because, as much as he might like an easy way out of the place in which he found himself now, something deep inside told him the best way out might be to walk straight through.

"Tell him yes." Boyd curled his fingers around the glass of tea he'd ordered for Laurel. "Because this is my home now."

~*~

Laurel pulled into a parking space in front of the Prickly Pear in time to see Boyd step into the diner. She cut the engine and watched through the plate glass window as he crossed the dining room to greet the beautiful woman who waited in a corner booth.

Boyd's former fiancée looked exactly as Laurel had pictured her: beautiful blonde hair styled to perfection; tall, trim figure clad in stylish, expensive-looking clothes—the kind Laurel admired in the magazines she read on her lunch break.

Boyd's ex—Annette—looked at him with such admiration that Laurel's chest began to ache. How could his head not be turned back toward such a beautiful woman, and one to whom he had already been close enough to want to marry? All he had to do was leave Blithe Settlement and go back to Houston. Karen would drop the lawsuit. None of the trouble he was having here would follow him there.

Annette wrapped her arms around Boyd's neck as his smile softened; betraying the fact that he still felt something for her.

Laurel swallowed against the growing ache in her throat as she watched Boyd's arms encircle the other woman, intimately familiar.

They looked perfect together.

Laurel glanced to the store apron on the seat beside her, then to the rearview mirror at the wanton hair barely contained by the braid that hung loosely over one shoulder. Why would he want her when he could have Annette?

A glance around the parking lot confirmed that no one had noticed her. Boyd certainly hadn't seen her yet, and for good reason. She could easily slip away without anyone knowing she'd been there, leaving Boyd to Annette and the former life that seemed to be drawing him back.

It would probably be for the best if she did. How long would Boyd's patience hold while he waited for her? He wanted to be married with a family, and she wasn't sure she wanted to ensnare herself in that way ever again. Marriage had been nothing but a source of pain and misery, for her and her sons. Now she was free; independent and self-sufficient. Maybe she didn't want to give that up.

And Boyd surely wouldn't be content to continue on, platonic as they were, indefinitely.

Not when Annette was so clearly still in love with him.

Laurel glanced again at the woman Boyd had once chosen. An ache welled in her heart so suddenly she pressed a hand to her chest in an attempt to quell it. She might not be willing to get married again. But one thing was certain: She loved Boyd like she'd never loved anyone else. He was good on a whole different level than anyone she'd ever met.

Laurel had stood by Tommy through the absolute worst circumstances—circumstances for which no one would have blamed her if she had left him.

What kind of foolish woman must Annette be to have let Boyd go simply because his professional life had taken a messy turn and she hadn't wanted to leave Houston?

Boyd glanced at the door and Laurel's heart skipped. He was looking for her. And she would not leave him like the other woman had done. If he chose Annette, so be it. But Laurel would stand by him until he asked her not to, in the same way he had stood beside her when she had suggested that all this legal mess could be solved if he would simply stop seeing her.

With a deep determined breath, Laurel stepped out of the car, pulled her cheap, dollar store handbag onto her shoulder, and headed to the diner's entrance.

The look of relief on Boyd's face when he saw her gave her flagging confidence a boost and filled her with a measure of peace. He stood and reached for her hand as she approached, then he let her slip into the booth before he slid in beside her.

~*~

"Thanks for going with me tonight."

Laurel nodded at Boyd's gratitude and pushed her front door open. He might not be so grateful if he knew how close she'd come to standing him up. But she wouldn't confess it. He'd been so relieved at her arrival that she'd been ashamed of herself for nearly succumbing to the fiery darts that had her believing he would be better off without her.

Boyd followed her inside and closed the door gently.

T.J. sat on the sofa watching television.

"I brought you and Joshua some dinner." Laurel held up the plastic bag containing burgers and fries for the boys.

Joshua jumped up from his spot on the floor, took the bag and headed for the kitchen.

T.J. was a little slower to rise, but when he did, Laurel was struck again by how much he'd grown. He was now a couple of inches taller than she was, and the timbre of his voice had deepened nearly to that of a man's. It cracked slightly as he thanked her for dinner.

Boyd crossed the tiny living room and dropped into the sofa, reaching for a copy of the local weekly paper on the coffee table. "Did you get a chance to read Sunday's paper?"

Laurel slipped off her jacket and hung it on the coat rack, then turned to face Boyd, sympathy welling.

The front page article was pretty vague on actual details, but it very clearly made the point that Boyd was being sued for the wrongful death of her husband.

And, while Boyd had refused to comment for the article, Karen had been free with her accusations, holding nothing back.

She had thought that most people in town already knew about the lawsuit. But evidently, that wasn't the case.

Or maybe Karen's side of the story had persuaded them to take her side.

Their reception at church on Sunday morning had been a little frosty, and Boyd had been quieter than normal since then.

Accustomed as she was to being treated like an outsider who belonged on the fringes of their community, she could let it roll off and not faze her.

But Boyd's struggle with the sudden notoriety made her heart ache.

"How has work been this week?" Laurel sat beside him, slipped her shoes off and tucked her socked feet underneath her.

He took a deep breath and let it out on a weary sigh. "Slow. We had a few cancellations."

She laid a hand on his shoulder.

"I thought by not settling this lawsuit, for seeing it through and standing up for what's actually true, that I might somehow be justified. But, justified or not, if patients leave me and I lose my practice..." He looked at her for a long moment.

Tense anxiety radiated from him and seeped more deeply into her. What if? "You've had cancellations before, right? Maybe today's cancellations didn't have anything to do with the lawsuit or the article in the paper. Maybe they were just coincidental."

Boyd took her hand, raised it to his mouth and

pressed a kiss to the back of it with a sigh. Then he nodded. "You're right. Maybe I'm reading too much into it. But this town isn't like Houston. I could have started over in Houston after the last lawsuit settled, but I came here thinking I wanted a fresh start. I couldn't start over here again. Everyone knows me."

"So, if you felt like you had to start over somewhere else, where would you go?" Laurel asked the question softly, not meeting his eyes, unsure she wanted to hear his answer. "Would you go back to Houston?"

Back to his old life. Back to Annette. Or would he ask her to go with him? And if he did, would she go?

Suddenly she understood his need to leave Houston and come here where no one had known him. The prospect appealed to her now as it never had before, regardless of the outcome of the lawsuit—win or lose, to leave Blithe Settlement behind along with all the pain that had lived here with her. But did she really want to?

"I don't know if I can start over again," he said after a long silence. "I don't know if I want to. But I don't know what else I would do."

Laurel touched the gently waving hair at his temple, not knowing how to comfort or counsel him.

"And in the midst of everything else going on, Annette chooses now to want to come through town and catch up."

"She couldn't have known what all you're dealing with now."

"Sure she did." Boyd laid his head against the sofa back and turned to face her. "She's still in touch with my parents. They told her all about it. Her timing was always pretty terrible."

"She seemed nice."

Annette's assessing gaze—startled and curious, but not unkind—had lingered on Laurel as Boyd introduced them to each other, and she had the grace to smile and offer to shake hands. But Laurel's presence had clearly been unanticipated. Still, Boyd's former fiancée had treated her with respect and courtesy.

Now Boyd nodded as his thoughts turned inward and he fell silent. He had so much on his mind. And now, in addition to Karen's lawsuit and patients cancelling appointments, his thoughts had turned back to his fiancée and Houston.

"Do you regret leaving Houston and coming here?" Laurel voiced the question softly, even though she already knew the answer.

How could he not regret it? He had admitted to years of feeling isolated and alone, on the fringes of this community simply because he wasn't from around here. And this lawsuit, brought against him by Karen Kerr, had been dragging on for six months now, and it had the potential to ruin him if the judge wasn't sympathetic when he finally heard the arguments.

Boyd turned his head and glanced away, his deep, troubled sigh saying more than any words could.

No doubt his life here was nothing more than one long string of regrets.

15

Boyd had prayed for long hours that it wouldn't come to this. He had petitioned God earnestly that this case would just end...that Karen would somehow, miraculously, see reason and drop her charges.

He took a seat against the wall, in the same position he'd been in when Karen's lawyer had deposed Laurel.

This time, however, T.J. sat in the hot seat. Bad enough he'd had to sit silently and listen to Laurel defend her actions with regard to Tommy. Now he would have to listen as T.J. told the same stories from his own perspective.

And Boyd knew how unpredictable a teenager's emotions could be, especially in times of high stress. Anything could happen.

T.J. sat stoically with Colin beside him. He turned and glanced back at Boyd, as if to make sure he was still there.

Boyd gave him a smile and a nod of encouragement.

Why did this need to feel so much like the kid and his mother were the ones on trial? If anyone was innocent of any wrongdoing in this situation, it was them. The whole world seemed backwards and upside down right now with the guilty accusing the innocent. A new wave of angry frustration swelled to twist his stomach into a knot.

Karen and her lawyer entered, and the woman's face contorted when she saw her grandson.

"T.J, what are you doing here? Why, son?"

"You tell me, Grandma?" T.J. responded coolly. "Why am I here?"

Boyd remained silent.

No doubt, Karen had hoped that her grandson would somehow refuse to be deposed, as if it were a possibility. But seeing him here now, seated across from her, she nearly crumbled into emotional hysterics. One might think she was the one being falsely accused; that it was her future that hung in the balance. Maybe that's exactly how she saw it. But Boyd had, in the past months, come to believe that Karen's emotional meltdowns were more for the purpose of manipulation than anything else.

"Do you need to wait outside?" Karen's counselor asked her.

Boyd glanced at Karen to measure her reaction. That would be the worst place for her to wait. Laurel was out in the lobby and Boyd would not sit in here while Karen sat out there with Laurel. At the same time, he didn't want to leave T.J. in here without him here for moral support.

But Karen didn't want to be in the lobby waiting. She would be able to influence nothing in here from out there.

Boyd closed his eyes and silently asked the Lord to fill his heart with mercy and grace for this woman. Karen didn't know the Lord. And she was only lashing out now at all of them in the midst of her own pain; grieving as those who have no hope.

"No." Karen sniffed and was dabbing her eyes as Boyd opened his. "No. I'll be fine."

The opposing counsel assessed his client almost skeptically for another moment, and then he turned his attention to the teenager across the table with a grim expression.

"So, T.J."

T.J. didn't respond.

"How is school going for you this year?"

"Fine."

"What grade are you in now?"

"Ninth."

The lawyer paused. It had to be as clear to him as it was to Boyd that T.J. had been coached well and didn't need a reason not to trust the man.

"Are you doing well in your classes?"

T.J. shrugged and nodded, relaxing. "Yes."

"Good. What's your favorite subject?

"I guess math."

The counselor nodded. "I was never any good at math. I guess I was always better with words. Why math? What makes it your favorite?"

Again, T.J. shrugged. "It's like working a puzzle or solving a riddle, I guess. It's cool to be able to start with a problem and find the solution. I like science, too."

The lawyer nodded and remained quiet for a long moment before continuing. "Ninth grade…I guess that means you'll need to be thinking about college in a couple of years. Do you have one in mind?"

T.J. shrugged and shook his head. "I never thought about it. I always kind of assumed I wouldn't go to college."

"Why not?"

"I don't know. We don't have a lot of money. My grades aren't good enough for a bunch of scholarships..."

"I don't know." The lawyer said. "It sounds to me as if you make decent grades. You might be surprised what kind of financial aid you'd get."

T.J. nodded slowly, but didn't speak.

"What about extracurricular activities? Are you playing any sports? Maybe football?"

"No."

"Why not?"

"Because I don't want to."

"Well, what kinds of things do you like to spend your free time doing?"

T.J. shrugged.

"Do you like video games?"

"I guess."

"Do you play video games a lot?"

"Yes."

"What kind of games to you play?"

T.J. shrugged again. "Sports games. Mostly I play the ones that my brother wants to play."

"Do you ever play the war games? Or the ones where you kill zombies?"

T.J. shook his head. "No."

"Really? My kids love those. Why don't you play those?"

"Mom doesn't like them."

"So she won't let you play them?"

"No."

"Do you know why she doesn't like them?"

"She says they're too violent."

"Does she?" There was no sarcasm or implied disbelief in the lawyer's tone.

"Yes. She thinks we've seen enough of that in our real life."

"In your real life…is that where you learned to use a real gun?"

T.J. didn't answer.

"Because that's where you violently pointed a shotgun at your father and threatened to shoot him, isn't it? In your real life?"

"Yes." T.J looked straight at the lawyer with an unnatural calm. "I pointed a shotgun at my father and threatened to shoot him. But why don't you ask me why I did that? Because if you did, I'd tell you it was because he was beating up my mother. Why does this lawsuit seem to only be about what my mother did, or what I did, or what Dr. Wendall didn't do? Why is it not about what my father did to get himself shot in the first place? And, just so you know, Grandma, the person who actually shot and killed Dad is already in jail."

For a moment, the only sound in the room came from the end of the table where the court reporter sat recording the words spoken.

"Did you love your father?"

T.J.'s steady stare faltered and he glanced to the table. "Of course I loved my father."

"Did you like him?"

"We weren't buddies, if that's what you're asking."

"Do you think he loved you?"

Boyd watched as T.J.'s back swelled with the deep breath he took and held for a long, silent moment.

Finally, he shook his head. "No. I don't think he loved anyone."

"You seem like a good kid, T.J. But it sounds to me as if you had a really rough home life. Most kids in your situation get into trouble, but you don't. Why is that, do you think?"

"Because of my mom." T.J. said it like it should be obvious. "She loves us. I watched her put herself between Joshua and my father to protect him. A hundred times, or maybe more, she's done the same thing for me. My father never made that kind of sacrifice for anyone. I guess I just didn't want to make her life any harder than it already was."

"Your brother called the police on him one night, is that right? And the police ended up arresting your father, right?"

"Yes. Ask me why."

T.J. held the man's gaze for a long moment until the lawyer took his glasses off and pinched the bridge of his nose. "Why?"

"Because he was beating up my mother, and I couldn't find the shotgun. And it's a good thing I couldn't because that night I would have shot him."

Colin quickly laid a hand on T.J.'s arm before the boy could say any more.

"Do you really think you could have done such a thing, T.J.?"

"Yes. That day I could have."

Karen's lawyer looked at Boyd for a long moment. This line of questioning would never work in Karen's favor unless her lawyer had some way of twisting the facts that Boyd couldn't imagine. Either the opposing counsel was the worst lawyer ever, or he was setting the stage to deliberately lose his case.

"Why that day?"

Boyd cast his gaze to his knees, knowing that this was a question the opposing counsel should avoid if at all possible.

"Because he said he was going to kill my mother,

and I believed him."

"So, you and your brother thought you could protect her?"

"Someone had to. Because he never did. It was his job to protect her—to protect us. But instead, he was the *thing* we needed protection from."

The counselor drew in a serious breath and pushed it out evenly, nodding slowly. "Had your father ever threatened to kill you or your mother before?"

"Not me, and not Joshua, as far as I know. But he threatened to kill Mom a few times before."

"Did you believe he would really do it?"

T.J. nodded. "When I was little, I'd lay in bed at night crying because I thought she'd be dead by morning. I wouldn't have threatened to shoot him if I didn't think he meant it."

"When he treated you guys this way, and when he made these threats, was he usually drunk or sober?"

"He was usually drunk. Period. But he was mean when he was sober, too."

Karen's histrionic displays had quieted during the deposition.

Boyd glanced her way to find her staring into the glossy veneer of the conference table, quiet for a change; no sniffling into a tissue dramatically, no *tsks* or grunts meant to communicate disgust and disbelief. But there was no true peace in her. He had the impression that this quiet moment was perhaps the eye of the storm that had been trying to blow them away for the better part of this year.

Maybe Karen had the same sense he did that her lawyer was steering this deposition in a direction that could not end well for her.

Colin must have had the same sense. He sat quietly beside T.J., staring at the legal pad on which he'd stopped taking notes and laid down his pen. He seemed to be letting T.J. simply say what he wanted to say.

Karen's lawyer had conducted Boyd's, and even Laurel's deposition, in a more antagonistic manner. But today, with T.J., he seemed to be taking a softer approach—a less beneficial approach for his case. But why?

"On that night," the other counselor began, "the night your brother called the police and your father went to jail, your mother ended up at the hospital, is that right?"

T.J. nodded. "Yes."

"Why did you call Dr. Wendall instead of your grandmother?"

T.J.'s back swelled with another deep breath. That was perhaps the question upon which the entire case hinged. "I didn't call my grandmother because I knew she wouldn't come." T.J. shook his head. "She would have been more worried about what my dad was going through in jail than what my mom was going through at the hospital. And I was right."

Karen's eyes had filled anew, but the tears fell silently this time.

"I called Dr. Wendall because he's a doctor. I knew he could help, and I knew he would."

"And that's the only reason?"

"Yes." T.J. said simply. "That's the only reason. He's the only person I know that I thought would help us."

After a long silence, the opposing counsel gathered papers and folders and packed them away into his briefcase. The deposition was over.

Karen stood without a word and left.

Colin stepped aside and engaged the other lawyer in a quiet conversation across the room.

"What's wrong?" T.J. turned to Boyd, his face ashen as he glanced back to the two lawyers. "Did I say something I shouldn't have?"

"No." Boyd laid a gentle hand on his shoulder. "You did fine. You did very well."

But the wheels in Boyd's mind were spinning furiously. This deposition had somehow been a turning point for the lawsuit, although he couldn't see exactly how.

The conversation across the room, carried out in hushed, almost urgent tones was alarming. The questions asked and answered in the last hour couldn't possibly help Karen's case—at least not as far as he could see.

But he didn't think in these terms. Maybe an offensive move was coming that would knock the feet out from underneath them.

Maybe the trap had been sprung, and he didn't even know he was caught yet.

~*~

"Are you sure you wouldn't rather just come over to our house and let me fix something for us?" Laurel tried to make the offer sound nonchalant. But she heard the note of concern in her own voice; surely Boyd heard it as well.

He intertwined his fingers with hers and raised her hand to his mouth, pressing a soft kiss to the back. "I'm sure." He pulled open the Prickly Pear door and held it for her, T.J., and Joshua. "I think a large supreme pizza is just what we need tonight."

"We could get our pizza to go."

He shook his head. "Let's eat here. I think we've been hiding out long enough."

She nodded. Hiding out wasn't unusual for her. She'd spent most of her life staying out of the way as much as possible. But she could understand how it might begin to wear on someone like Boyd who had never felt a need to avoid the world.

And the curious, sympathetic, and even skeptical gazes of the people around him were bound to be wearing very thin.

He should not have to hide away because he had been at the scene and offered what help he could when Tommy had been shot.

The Prickly Pear wasn't crowded this evening, but a dozen heads turned when they entered. A dozen gazes followed them inquisitively until they had tucked themselves into a side booth.

"How was work today?" Laurel spread a napkin across her lap. "Has traffic picked up again?"

Boyd nodded. "It has, actually. I hadn't really thought about it until now, but work has been busier these past couple of weeks. Someone—a patient— asked me today how the lawsuit was going. She wanted to know if I thought I would win." An ironic chuckle broke free. "Like it's a contest, or a game."

Laurel smiled. "She cares about you."

"Or maybe she's just nosy." T.J.'s interjection had the slightest edge of bitterness to it.

"Maybe." Boyd said. "But I like to think she was concerned for me. For all of us."

"So what did you tell her?" Joshua accepted a

glass of water from the waitress who quickly took their order and moved on.

"I told her that I didn't know." He grew silent for a moment, lost in a thought he clearly wasn't going to share. "But let's talk about something else." He glanced at T.J., who had seemed sullen since the deposition ended a couple of hours ago. "So, T.J., your favorite subject is math?"

That got a slight grin from him. "It is now that I understand it, and now that I know I can do it and I'm not stupid. I think my teacher thinks I'm cheating."

"Why do you think that?" Laurel checked her impulse to assume the worst about T.J's teacher. She'd tried hard this year to be objective and see the man's side of the issues present. But he seemed to have some kind of personal grudge against T.J., and she couldn't fathom why. Or maybe she could. The family the boys came from was enough to influence any respectable person's opinion against them.

T.J. shrugged. "I've made A's on all my homework since Dr. Wendall's been helping me. He keeps making comments about it, like, 'Well, looky there, T.J., another A. All of a sudden you're a regular straight A student.'"

Boyd smiled at T.J.'s puffed-up impersonation of his teacher.

But Laurel was not amused. "Have you explained to him that you've been getting help from someone who could actually *teach* math to you? Someone who actually cares whether or not you understand it?"

Boyd's smile widened further at her defensive response.

"No, Mom." T.J. smiled freely now. "I didn't think I should say something like that to a teacher. Besides, I know I'm not cheating. I don't care what he thinks."

Admiration swelled for this boy—fourteen, and nearly a man. Laurel swallowed as her ruffled feathers smoothed.

T.J. was being falsely accused, and he had handled it, and likely much more, with a quiet strength that was rare in adults.

"T.J., I think it's time that you and Joshua started calling me something besides Dr. Wendall." Boyd made the announcement as if he'd just thought of it.

Both boys stared at him, dumbstruck.

"Like what?" Laurel asked.

"How about Boyd?"

The boys glanced from him to her, as if for permission.

"Won't that be a little weird when we're sick and we come to your office?" Joshua grabbed for a slice of pizza as the waitress delivered it to their table.

Boyd extended his hands, one to Laurel and the other across the table to T.J. The four joined hands, and then he offered a soft blessing over their meal. "Yes." He picked the conversation back up and reached for his own slice. "That would be weird. Which is why we need to find you guys a new doctor."

"What?" T.J. sounded as if the breath had been knocked out of him.

"Why?" Joshua protested a bit too loudly.

Boyd glanced at Laurel long enough, she was sure, to note the alarm that must show plainly on her face. Then he continued gently. "Doctors don't treat their own families. It's something of a conflict of interest, and we can't always be as clinical and objective as we need to be. So, unless it's an emergency, it's a practice we try to avoid."

The boys looked at him, then at each other.

"And I guess I'm starting to think of you guys as family. I hope that's OK with you. I love you guys. And I love your mom, too."

Heat rose to Laurel's cheeks and her eyes filled.

"I thought I'd wait to suggest the new doctor thing until after the lawsuit was finished, but we don't even have an official court date yet. And if Karen wins, I'll probably appeal it. It could be years before it's finally resolved."

T.J.'s grin, which had been slowly widening, slackened a bit and he looked at his plate.

"I don't want everything else about our lives to be on hold indefinitely until this is over. So, I'd like you guys to start calling me Boyd—if it's OK with your mom."

Both boys looked to her for the word that would allow them to take one step closer to this man they admired so much. Boyd was the first man they'd ever trusted, and she understood completely how they felt. He was the first man she'd ever trusted. How could she tell them no?

Their expressions told her plainly how badly they wanted to let Boyd into their lives in this way, as well as how much they wanted to become a part of his. What would be the point of not allowing it?

So many times she'd worried about the impact her involvement with Boyd might have on her boys, especially if that involvement were to end. But nearly a year had passed since their father's death. She'd often thought that she might not want to relinquish her freedom, now that she had achieved it. But by marrying again, she knew now that what she'd really been afraid of was entangling herself with another man like Tommy. Marriage to Boyd could never become such a thing.

But more than that, she wouldn't really be protecting her boys from anything by insisting that they keep a distance from Boyd based on artificial formality. Their hearts were already connected with his, and while she had been able to protect them to some degree from their father's violence, she couldn't stop life from potentially breaking their hearts. And she didn't want to stop them from loving Boyd any more than she could stop herself.

With a nod to her boys, she opened the door to a new future.

Boyd's answering smile said that he understood the implication.

"Good. That's settled." Boyd pushed his plate away, signaled to the waitress for the check, and then glanced from Joshua to T.J. "Who's up for a game of Monopoly?"

Boyd opened his wallet and pulled out a generous tip, glancing around again for the waitress who seemed to have disappeared. He rose and headed for the cash register followed closely by T.J.

Joshua hung back with her as she piled napkins together and rose to follow. He wanted to say something, this quiet, sensitive child of hers. Joshua felt things deeply and was always analyzing every situation. He knew better than anyone what a big step it had been for her to allow them to call Boyd by his first name. But, although he clearly had something to say about it, he remained quiet, still processing his thoughts and emotions.

Laurel put an arm around his shoulders and gave a gentle squeeze as they joined Boyd and T.J. at the cash register.

"...already paid by who?" Boyd was asking.

"By an anonymous friend," the young cashier answered. "That's all I was told to tell you. And he left you this note."

Boyd accepted the folded slip of paper. "Thank you."

"Don't thank me." The girl behind the counter said with a shrug and a grin.

He unfolded the note, swallowing hard as a soft puzzled smile emerged. Then he handed the paper to Laurel.

"We are praying for you." That's all it said.

Boyd's phone rang as they stepped out into the crisp, early evening air.

Colin's name lit the display.

Boyd answered and then listened quietly for a long moment.

He tensed, and Laurel laid a hand on his arm, waiting to hear the news, whatever it was, and sensing by Boyd's reaction that it wasn't good.

Boyd thanked Colin and ended the call, then looked at her.

"Is it bad?" T.J. asked.

Boyd shook his head slowly. "It's not anything I didn't expect. I had hoped after today's deposition that Karen would drop the lawsuit, but she hasn't. They've scheduled the hearing for January."

16

Laurel stepped out of the new sport utility crossover as Boyd opened the door for her.

T.J. and Joshua got out of the back, and then all four stood for a moment gazing up at the imposing façade of the courthouse that loomed before them, dismal as ever—especially given the winter bare trees, dormant lawn, and cold, overcast sky.

She pressed a hand to her midsection in a vain attempt to quell the mounting nerves. She'd grown to detest this building.

But today would be a good day—how could it not be, and Boyd's encouraging smile calmed her. He was sure about this, and she needed no more convincing to believe that, after today, their life together could finally begin for real.

"Are you guys ready?"

T.J. and Joshua nodded in unison.

"And you're sure about this? This is what you want to do?"

"Yes sir." T.J. answered for both as Joshua nodded again.

Boyd turned to Laurel. "OK, then. Let's go. I'll bet Colin is already waiting inside for us."

In fact, Colin was ready and waiting just inside the security check point. His easy smile set Laurel further at ease. He had been confident from the beginning that this proceeding would go smoothly, and he should know.

Colin shook Boyd's hand, then T.J.'s, and finally Joshua's. Then he greeted her with a kiss on the cheek. In the past year, he had become more than simply their legal counsel. He was their friend—and a handy friend to have.

"Court is a little ahead of schedule today." Colin turned and led them down the corridor toward the courtroom that had been the source of her nightmares in recent months. "Judge Fowler can see us now if y'all are ready." He paused at the door and turned expectantly. "Are we ready?"

Blinking back misty tears—willing herself not to let them spill, Laurel straightened the collar of T.J.'s dress shirt as he nodded. She placed trembling hands on Joshua's shoulders.

"We're ready, Mom." He assured her. "And it's what we want to do."

She nodded, but no words came.

The courtroom was empty except for the judge, who sat silently leafing through pages laid out in front of him. He didn't look up as they entered.

Laurel shed her coat along with the others, laid it over the back of a chair, and then glanced warily back at the bench.

Judge Fowler was a bit of a curmudgeon, and there was no way to predict the outcome of today's hearing.

But Colin was certain.

And so were Boyd and the boys.

Laurel approached the bench and stood beside Boyd, who interlaced his fingers with hers. The warmth of his hand spread blessedly through her, calming her.

"What's the occasion?" Judge Fowler's brusque query drove Laurel's gaze to the floor. "Have you all just come from a funeral or a wedding?"

She glanced up at Boyd. He still had his boutonniere pinned to his lapel. So did Colin. Not the boys, however. They'd probably ripped theirs off at the first opportunity. The blue silk of her own dress, while not formal by any means, probably was a little dressier than the judge usually saw in his courtroom.

"A wedding, Your Honor." Colin answered.

"Oh? Whose?"

"Ours." Boyd glanced at Laurel and then gave her a wink and an easy smile that accentuated the cleft in his chin.

"I didn't hear anything about a wedding today."

"It was a small, private ceremony." Boyd responded. "Just us and a few other friends in the pastor's study."

Laurel linked an arm through Boyd's, remembering his softly spoken vow to love, honor, and cherish her for the rest of his life. The sincerity of his expression told her that he meant every word, and that she would never again fear violence from the man who was supposed to protect her.

She glanced back up at the judge to find him staring for a moment, almost as if he thought it was a joke and he was waiting for the punch line. When it didn't come, he adjusted his glasses and turned his attention to the papers laid out in front of him.

"And now you, Dr. Boyd Wendall, want to adopt these boys?"

"Yes sir." Boyd answered.

"And that's OK with their mother?" Judge Fowler turned his heavily browed gaze to her.

"Yes sir." She pushed the response through her constricted throat.

"And it's OK with the boys here?" He turned to them.

"Yes sir." They spoke in unison.

Judge Fowler nodded as his gaze swept over them all once more.

"What does your mother-in-law think about this, Mrs. Kerr—I'm sorry, Mrs. Wendall?"

Laurel drew in a deep breath, regret surfacing with her reply.

"I don't know, Your Honor. We haven't spoken with her since the hearing ended. Not because we haven't tried. She just won't take my calls. She won't answer the door when we come by. So, I suspect this decision won't make her the least bit happy."

Judge Fowler gave a small grunt that might have been intended as an ironic laugh, or maybe hearty agreement.

Indeed, it would be another item in a long list of things that made Karen unhappy. Laurel's mother-in-law's bitter loneliness grieved her heart. But the woman had done it to herself through the choices she'd made. And she seemed to have no desire to be reconciled to the family she had remaining. Still, Laurel would not quit trying—at least not yet.

Far from splitting Laurel and Boyd up, as had been her intention, Karen's lawsuit had only served to knit them more closely together. That ordeal had been the very thing that had bonded Laurel, Boyd, T.J. and Joshua as a family. Karen had succeeded in achieving the exact opposite outcome she'd intended.

Although her lawyer had tried to convince Karen to drop the suit, she continued to flail blindly in her rage and bitterness, unable to see that she had no case. So she pressed on. But Laurel and the boys had not even been called to testify.

Boyd had taken the stand, but the testimony of the paramedics had destroyed Karen's charges. And what no one had known was that the police who responded that night had immediately requested, and still had as evidence, the convenience store's security video of the parking lot and the inside of the store the night Tommy died.

Colin had guessed there'd be one, and requested it.

Everyone had watched not only what Tommy and his blonde girlfriend bought, but the entire sequence in the parking lot.

The hearing had taken two hours. Judge Fowler himself had dismissed the proceeding with a scathing, humiliating commentary for Karen.

It had made Laurel's heart ache as she watched.

But that was all over.

Today, she had married Boyd. Now, he was adopting her sons. By tonight, they would legally be the family they already were in their hearts.

"So what's next, Dr. Wendall?" The judged asked.

"Peace and quiet, hopefully." Boyd squeezed her hand.

Judge Fowler grunted again. Then, with a flourish of his pen, he signed the papers in front of him.

Joshua went up on his toes, trying to see the signed papers.

Judge Fowler held them up for his inspection. "Can you see it, young man? It's official. You're now Joshua William Wendall, and your brother is Thomas Jeffrey Wendall. It's that easy."

But it had been anything but easy. And Laurel was not so naïve as to believe that life would be nothing but easy from here on. It would, however, be blessedly peaceful and joyful. For her entire life Laurel had felt as if God was unreachable, that she was unloved and unlovable, especially by a God who was so big and powerful and perfect—even since professing him as her savior. Though she had committed to Christ years before, she still was a babe in the woods when reaching out to her Lord. But in the past year and a half, she had drawn nearer to God.

Boyd had shown her how.

And God had drawn near to her, just as His word promised.

And now she knew, without a doubt and from experience, that her Savior was not so very far away at all.

~*~

The breeze off the water was chilly this afternoon, but that hadn't stopped T.J. and Joshua from running down to the beach the moment they caught sight of the gulf.

Laurel pulled her sweater closed and leaned against the deck rail, surveying the low clouds and busy waves, agitated by the early spring cold front that had stirred them up.

Boyd handed her a mug of steaming coffee as he joined her.

"I can't believe your family owns a house right on the beach." Laurel accepted the hot drink, letting it warm her hands for a moment before taking a sip.

"We used to come out here a few times a year."

Boyd sipped his coffee, and then took a seat on a sturdy wicker settee. "I always had a good time. Galveston is far enough away from Houston to make it feel like a vacation, and close enough to get back fast if my father needed to. I thought it would be a good place to spend spring break."

They had a house, on Galveston Island. Right on the beach.

Laurel almost couldn't comprehend such a thing.

But the sound of the wind and waves was real. The seagulls floating overhead crying out to the boys below were equally genuine. And, though it seemed like something only possible in a story—a fairy tale, now it all belonged to her as well.

"What are they doing down there?" Boyd squinted as if to bring Joshua and T.J. into better focus. "They're just...standing there, looking at it."

"They've never seen the ocean before." Laurel gently set her coffee on an end table and joined him on the sofa.

He wrapped a warm arm around her shoulders. Boyd glanced briefly at her, then back out to her sons—their sons, mystified.

"I've never seen it either." She let the admission come softly as she rested her head on his shoulder. "It looks as if it never ends. That's probably what has them so spellbound."

T.J. and Joshua turned and began walking along the shore. One adamant wave reached farther up onto the beach than the rest, making both boys scurry to avoid it, as if it might pull them back into the gulf with it.

"I told them to stay within sight of the house for now."

She nodded and closed her eyes, letting the sound of the water lull her for a long moment.

"Thank you," she whispered.

He chuckled. "You're welcome."

"No, I mean thank you for this. For everything. For not settling the lawsuit and for not letting me push you away so you didn't have to go through it. Thank you for carrying a burden that didn't have anything to do with you, and for being so steady all those times when you ended up in the middle of my messy life, and for not hating Karen no matter how hatefully she treats you. Thank you for adopting T.J. and Joshua…" Laurel let her voice trail off as gratitude and love for this man nearly overwhelmed her.

He seemed to sense the intensity of her emotions, and he pulled her a little closer and pressed a kiss to the top of her head.

"You didn't have to do it." Laurel could barely voice the thought. "And we still would have been perfectly happy if you hadn't. But you did, and that it was your idea…it just means so much to all of us."

"I wanted them to know that I'm as committed to them as I am to you."

Laurel nodded and raised her head as her sons turned and came back up the beach toward the house.

"I remember a conversation the boys and I had after Tommy died…about a passage in the Bible—in Exodus—that talks about how He punishes children and their children for the sins of their fathers. They wanted to know what that idea might mean for them, and I couldn't explain it." She looked up into his kind, green eyes and couldn't suppress a smile. "But you're their father now, Boyd. And I'm hoping maybe they will see that and know that God has wiped the slate clean for them." She laid her head on his shoulder again and let a contented sigh slip free. "So, thank you."

"You are more than welcome." Boyd pressed another warm kiss to her temple. "And thank you, too."

She smiled, knowing full well that she had gained the most from their marriage. "For what?"

"For finally calling me Boyd."

She glanced up at him to confirm that he was teasing.

"For years all I ever heard from anybody was Dr. Wendall." He grinned.

She matched his smile.

"Dr. Wendall this, and Dr. Wendall that. And I'd tell everyone I knew to call me Boyd, but no one ever would, except Justin Barnet. There were only two things I've really wanted since coming to Blithe Settlement; for people to call me by my first name, and to have a family. And you have given me both of those. So, thank you."

"Mom!" T.J.'s voice reached her on the wind.

She and Boyd rose and stepped to the deck rail to see both boys on the beach below waving at them.

"Come down and see it."

Laurel glanced at Boyd, questioning.

"You said you've never seen it before either." He took her hand and led her to the stairs. "You should at least get your feet wet."

"Won't it be cold?"

"Yes."

Joshua and T.J. greeted them as they reached the bottom.

"Come on, Mom." Joshua's breathless enthusiasm

made her smile.

Laurel stepped off the stairs and into the sand, letting Boyd lead her toward the edge of the water as the sea breeze tugged strands of her hair loose.

The boys kicked off their shoes and charged ahead into the water until they were up to their knees, whooping and shouting about the gulf's shocking chill.

Laurel slipped off her sandals and followed.

God had given her what she needed. They were a family.

Thank you

We appreciate you reading this White Rose Publishing title. For other inspirational stories, please visit our on-line bookstore at www.pelicanbookgroup.com.

For questions or more information, contact us at customer@pelicanbookgroup.com.

White Rose Publishing
Where Faith is the Cornerstone of Love™
an imprint of Pelican Ventures Book Group
www.PelicanBookGroup.com

Connect with Us
www.facebook.com/Pelicanbookgroup
www.twitter.com/pelicanbookgrp

To receive news and specials, subscribe to our bulletin
http://pelink.us/bulletin

May God's glory shine through
this inspirational work of fiction.

AMDG

Free Book Offer

We're looking for booklovers like you to partner with us! Join our team of influencers today and receive at least one free eBook per month. Maybe more!

For more information
Visit http://pelicanbookgroup.com/booklovers
or e-mail
booklovers@pelicanbookgroup.com

Don't Miss The Other Books In Series!
Available Now

Perfect Shelter

"Curse God and die!"

That's the advice Job got from his wife, and it sounds good to Elaine Mallory. After a life spent seeking and doing God's will, the course of one turbulent spring strips her of everything but her life. Maybe she's not quite inclined to curse God and die, but she's got no problem turning from Him and running hard in the opposite direction.

Justin Barnet wants nothing more than to comfort Elaine and shelter her from more suffering. Her loss and departure leaves him devastated, and for years he waits for her return–years during which his own life falls apart. Now Elaine is back, and he has less to offer than ever.

As Elaine faces her grief for the first time since that tragic spring, will it reopen her heart to God's perfect shelter–and to Justin? Or will it drive her away again?

Return to Me

Audrey Rhodes once walked the straight and narrow, but a terrible mistake changed the direction her life. Now former boyfriend and bad boy, Brent Thomason, is back in Blithe Settlement claiming newfound faith in God. Audrey's feelings for Brent haven't changed, but she has. Her life is in shambles. How can she be worthy of this new Brent's love?

Brent Thomason isn't proud of his past. Audrey had been his friend and his love, and he betrayed her. Now a veterinarian, he's returned home to work with Audrey's dad and make restitution for his misdeeds. Brent finds it's not so easy for people to accept his changed ways; still he must make things right with those he hurt, starting with Audrey.

As God directs their paths, Audrey discovers forgiveness is a two-edged sword...especially when she must first forgive herself. And Brent must accept God's will...even if it means losing Audrey a second time.

Moving On

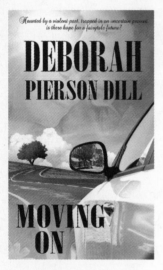

Meagan Layne longs for a traditional life as a wife and mother. Love, marriage to an honorable man, a stable home life for her son, more children; it shouldn't be too much to ask. So how did she end up divorced from a man who left her in debt, with a small son to support on a budget that barely meets at the ends?

Bobby Kerr despises his past and wants to build on the new start he made when he left his small hometown for Lubbock. He's a new man in Christ, but he can't forget the violent man he was. He won't subject another woman to the perils of life with him. But Meagan stirs Bobby's heart in a dangerous way, making him hope that love could be possible for him after all. If she's willing to risk it.